직선과 독가스
―병동에서

도서출판 아시아에서는 《바이링궐 에디션 한국 현대 소설》을 기획하여 한국의 우수한 문학을 주제별로 엄선해 국내외 독자들에게 소개합니다. 이 기획은 국내외 우수한 번역가들이 참여하여 원작의 품격을 최대한 살렸습니다. 문학을 통해 아시아의 정체성과 가치를 살피는 데 주력해 온 도서출판 아시아는 한국인의 삶을 넓고 깊게 이해하는 데 이 기획이 기여하기를 기대합니다.

Asia Publishers present some of the very best modern Korean literature to readers worldwide through its new Korean literature series 〈Bi-lingual Edition Modern Korean Literature〉. We are proud and happy to offer it in the most authoritative translation by renowned translators of Korean literature. We hope that this series helps to build solid bridges between citizens of the world and Koreans through rich in-depth understanding of Korea.

바이링궐 에디션 한국 현대 소설 018

Bi-lingual Edition Modern Korean Literature 018

Straight Lines and Poison Gas
—At the Hospital Wards

임철우

직선과 독가스
-병동에서

Lim Chul-woo

ASIA
PUBLISHERS

Contents

직선과 독가스
—병동에서

Straight Lines and Poison Gas
—At the Hospital Wards

한번 믿어보시라구요? 선생님을, 제가 말씀입니까? 방금 틀림없이 저한테 그렇게 말씀하신 것 같은데, 맞지요? 분명 제 귀가 옳게 들은 거지요? 으흐흐흐. 믿어달라, 믿어주시오…… 거참, 그럴듯한 얘깁니다. 뭐랄까, 하여튼 어째 약간 우스운 얘기를 제게 하고 계시는 것 같구먼요. 왜냐면 나는 늘 어떤 누군가가 또 다른 누군가를 믿는다는 일은 대단히 위험천만하고 무분별한 모험이라고 여기고 있으니까요. 그래요. 그것은 아주 어리석고도 위험스런 도박이지요. 이를테면, 캄캄한 밤중에(달도 없고 별조차 돋아나지 않는 그런 칠흑 같은 어둠 속 말입니다) 첩첩 깊은 산골짜기에서 우연히도 낯모르는 두 사람이 서로 딱 마주쳤

Trust you? I should, Doctor? I could swear that's what you just said, isn't it? I did hear you correctly, right? Heh haha. Believe me. Trust me... Boy, what a thing to say. How should I put it, you seem to be telling me something a bit funny somehow. Because I always think it's a most dangerous and undiscerning venture for a person to trust another. Yes, it is a very foolish and dangerous gamble. As reckless and perilous as coming upon a stranger on a dark night—you know, in pitch-black darkness with no moon and no stars out—and willingly handing over to that person a knife with a sharp blade. In order to borrow—well, to take, really—the knife from

을 때, 한쪽 사람이 다른 쪽 사람에게 시퍼렇게 날 세운 칼 한 자루를 순순히 넘겨주는 것만큼이나 무모하고 위태로운 일이니까요. 칼을 빌리기 위해서, 아니 사실은 빼앗기 위해서지만, 한쪽 사람은 언제나 상대편과 눈을 맞춘 채 천연스레 웃어 보이면서 "믿어주시오, 제발" 하고 말하는 법입니다. 이제 막 선생님께서 내게 했던 바로 그대로 말입니다. 으흐흐. 대부분의 사람들은 그럴 경우엔 마음이 오뉴월 엿물처럼 흐늘흐늘해져서 의심을 풀고 말지도 모르죠. 하지만 나는 다르다 이 말씀입니다. 그 태연스러운 웃음에 맘이 약해져서 일단 칼자루를 저쪽에게 넘겨주고 나면, 바로 그 순간부터 모든 사정은 완전히 백팔십도로 달라지게 되고 말 것임을 나는 잘 알고 있으니까요. 그 칼자루가 약속대로 원래의 주인에게 순순히 돌아오느냐, 아니면 오히려 그 음흉스런 칼끝이 주인의 심장을 노리고 추호의 망설임도 없이 곧장 날아들어 오느냐를 결정하는 것은 이제부터는 칼을 쥔 저쪽이기 때문입니다. 그러니까 결국 살해자와 살해를 당하는 사람을 확실히 선택하는 일은 다름 아닌 그 한 자루의 칼이 결정하는 셈이지요. 생각해보시라구요. 일단 칼자루를 넘겨받은 쪽이 아까와 같이 먼저 믿어주십시오라고 말하지 않을 것은 뻔한

you, the other person will always look you straight in the eye with an innocuous-looking smile and say, "Trust me, please." Like you did with me just now. Heh haha. Most people in that situation may soften their defenses like summer honey and let go of their suspicion. But I'm telling you I'm different. Because I know only too well that once your heart softens up from that carefree smile and you hand over the knife to the other side, everything turns one hundred and eighty degrees. Because from then on it is the other side, holding the knife, who decides whether the knife is returned to the original owner as promised, or whether it comes back with its tip pointed straight at the owner's heart without hesitation. So, in a way, it is the knife that clearly decides who gets to murder and who gets murdered. Think about it. It's clear as day that the side that's already been handed the knife will no longer say, "Please trust me," as before. The moment the knife is in his hand, the guy, with his eyes glaring, will smugly give orders like this: trust me. You have to trust me. Or you'll regret it. Heh haha. And now you're asking me to trust you, Doctor. Heh heh. Isn't this too funny?

I mean, those people told me the same thing as

노릇이잖습니까. 칼자루가 손에 들어오는 순간부터 그쪽은 눈을 홉뜨며 이렇게 당당하게 명령할 테니까요. "믿어라. 믿어야 해. 그렇잖으면 넌 후회하게 될 거야." 하고 말입니다. 으흐흐. 그런데 선생님께서 내게 믿어보라고 하시다니, 흐흐, 거. 어째 우스운 일이잖습니까.

하기야 그자들도 선생님과 똑같은 말을 내게 했었습니다만. 아, 맞았습니다. 좀 전에 나를 이리로 데려다주고 나가버린 그 매부리코 녀석도 그자들과 한패지요. 사흘 동안이나(아냐 어쩌면 닷새일지도 몰라) 잠 한숨 편히 재워주지 않은 놈들이라구요. 아아, 지독한 자식들 같으니라구. 난 아예 이 두 눈알이 군밤처럼 지글지글 익어버린 줄만 알았다니까요. 참 이상하지 뭡니까. 내 얼굴만을 노리고 똑바로 쏟아붓는 그 동그란 전등의 불빛을 잠시만 보고 있노라면 금방 눈알이 터져버릴 것처럼 아파오면서 도대체 아무것도 뵈지가 않는 것이었습니다. 마치 숯불이 이글이글 타고 있는 아궁이 속에다가 통째로 머리통을 쑤셔박고 나자빠져 있는 듯한 지긋지긋한 느낌이 들더라니까요. 지금 당장이라도 내 머리통을 두 쪽으로 쪼개어놓고 들여다보면 어쩌면 그 속이 온통 찐고구마 꼴로 망가져 있을는지도 모르지요. 정말이지 이 며칠 동안은 난 영

12

you. Oh, right. That hooked nose who brought me here a moment ago and left is one of them, too. Those bastards didn't let me sleep comfortably once in as many as three—or perhaps it was five—days. Man, what S.O.B.s. I was sure my two eyes were totally scorched like roasted chestnuts. It's so weird. After a couple of seconds of staring at the round light bulb beaming straight at my face, my eyes would start to hurt like they were going to burst right there. And I wouldn't be able to see anything at all. It felt so tiresome, like my entire head was stuck in an oven with burning coals. Who knows, if you split open my head in two and look in there, maybe it'll be all cooked like steamed sweet potatoes. I tell you, I was no different from a mutt these past few days. One minute they'd be sweet-talking me, then bark at me the next, or bully me then act like they were lulling a crying baby... and even light my cigarette and whisper, "Hey, stop this nonsense and let's all be friends, huh? Trust me. Let's trust each other, let's try that. I trust you, you trust me. Like that." Ha, those manipulative bastards. But I didn't fall for it. Because there was a bad breath from their mouths, every single one of them. A foul, truly foul odor. You know, the smell of poison gas.

락없는 잡종개나 마찬가지 신세였습니다. 어르다가는 윽박지르고, 우격다짐을 하다가도 이내 살살 우는 애 달래는 시늉을 하고…… 그러다가는 또 친절하게 담배에 불까지 붙여 건네주면서 은근히 속삭이듯 말하는 것이었습니다. "이봐. 우리 그러지 말고 서로 친해보자구, 응. 믿어봐. 한번 눈 딱 감고 서로 믿어보는 거야. 난 당신을 믿고 당신은 날 믿고, 이렇게 말이야." 츳. 교활한 놈들. 하지만 난 속지 않았죠. 그자들의 입에선 하나같이 냄새가 났기 때문입니다. 지독한, 정말 지독한 냄새. 그 독가스 냄새 말입니다. 네? 모르시겠다니요. 아니, 그 끔찍한 독가스 냄새를 아직도 모르고 있다는 겁니까. 거 참 믿어지지 않는데요. 선생님 같은 의사가 모르면 누가 알겠습니까. 그 지독한 냄새 때문에 난 한시라도 목이 잠겨 숨을 쉴 수가 없는데…… 원 참, 그럴 리가.

좋습니다. 그렇다면 독가스 얘긴 그만두기로 하죠. 선생님도 역시 다른 사람들처럼 내 말을 믿어주지 않으려는 게 틀림없으니까…… 아니, 일부러 변명하실 필요까지는 없습니다. 그렇게 속이 뻔하게 드러나 보일 정도로 내 속마음을 떠보려고 공연히 애쓰지는 마시라구요. 그자들도 역시 며칠 동안이나 노력을 했지만 끝내 내게서 아무 자

What? You don't know? Why, are you saying you still don't know about that awful smell of poison gas? Wow, I can't believe it. If you don't know it and you're a doctor, who would know then? My throat is always hoarse because of that smell and I can't breathe... Oh, man, how do you not know it?

Fine. I'll stop talking about the poison gas, then. Like everyone else, I'm sure, you don't intend to ever believe me... No, you don't have to apologize. I mean, don't try so hard to get at what's on my mind in such a transparent way. They did their best for days, too, yet they couldn't get any confession— yes, they used the word "confession"—out of me. Isn't that what led them to drag me all the way here today? Crazy bastards. Actually, they were no longer confident they could get the better of me. Basically, I came out a winner. Hahah. "Don't lie. Why do you keep acting like a lunatic? Poison gas? What idiot on earth would believe bull like that? Tell me. What was your real intent? What gave you the nerve to dare to pull such crap without trepidation? Not to mention smack dab in the middle of Chungjang-ro of all places, crawling with people?" They took turns showing up day and night with all kinds of ruses and tactics, but I managed to keep my mouth

백도 (그래요. 그자들은 '자백'이라고 말했습니다) 받아내지 못하고 말았으니까요. 그 때문에 나를 오늘 이렇듯 여기까지 끌고 온 것이 아닙니까. 미친 짜아식들. 사실, 놈들은 더 이상 나를 이겨낼 자신이 없어진 것이죠. 결국 내가 승리한 셈입니다. 흐흣. "거짓말 마. 왜 자꾸만 미친놈 흉내를 내려는 거야. 독가스라니. 그따위 허튼소리를 믿을 등신이 세상에 누가 있어. 말해. 당신 진짜 속셈이 뭐였지. 무엇 때문에 겁대가리 없이 감히 그따위 허튼수작을 하고 있었던 거냐구. 그것도 하필이면 인파로 물 끓는 듯한 충장로 한가운데에서 말야." 그자들은 며칠 낮 며칠 밤을 번갈아 가며 나타나서는 온갖 술수와 계략을 다 부렸지만 난 용케도 입을 열지 않았지요. 혓바닥을 어금니로 꽉 깨물어 참고 또 참아냈습니다. 그렇다고 내가 무슨 옛날 어느 독립투사나 암살에 실패한 자객처럼 혓바닥을 끊어가면서까지 반드시 지켜야만 될 어떤 중대한 비밀 따위가 있어서가 아닙니다. 하긴, 어쩌면 그자들이 그 비슷하게 잘못 여기고 있었던 까닭에 그렇듯 나를 끈질기게 물고 늘어지려고 했었는지 어쨌는지는 잘 모르겠습니다만, 사실은 내가 끝끝내 입을 다물고 있었던 이유야 알고 보면 간단합니다. 모두가 다 그 독가스 탓이었으니까요. 참

shut. I persevered, biting down on my tongue with my back teeth. And I didn't have some huge secret that I absolutely had to keep like an old revolutionary activist or an assassin who failed in a mission, going so far as biting off my tongue or anything. Come to think of it, I don't know if that's what they thought, mistakenly, and that's why they were so doggedly persistent with me. But actually there's a simple reason why I didn't say anything until the end. It was all because of that poison gas. It was truly a foul stench. I could smell that nasty gas coming out of their mouths, with teeth stained yellow from tobacco tar, and their clothes, and that dammed stench was embedded in every corner of that room painted completely white. Sticky and clammy, it was smeared everywhere: over the metal chair I was sitting in that would make noises as if bones were grinding with one another, the plain square desk, the hanging light bulb that almost touched your head, the concrete floor, the doorknob, and so on. If you were to open up your hand and give one swipe as you might if you came home after a long trip, you could almost see black powder from the poison gas thickly rubbing off on your palm. Once, I asked them if it wasn't a gas cham-

말 지독한 냄새였습니다. 그자들의 누렇게 담뱃진이 박힌 입 안에서도 옷에서도 그 고약한 가스 냄새가 풀풀 풍겨져 나왔고, 온통 하얗게 칠한 네모진 방구석 어디를 둘러봐도 그 지긋지긋한 냄새가 짙게 배어 있었지요. 내가 앉은, 그 삐걱삐걱 뼈마디 부딪치는 듯한 소리를 내곤 하던 철제 의자와 사각형의 단조로운 책상, 머리가 닿을 정도로 낮게 드리워져 있는 전등, 그리고 콘크리트 바닥, 출입문 손잡이 할 것 없이 어디나 끈적하고 눅진하게 묻어 있어서, 우리가 오래 집을 비워둔 후에 돌아오면 으레 그러하듯이, 손바닥을 펴서 한 번만 쓱 문질러보면 금방이라도 수북한 먼지 같은 독가스의 분말이 꺼멓게 묻어 나올 것만 같았습니다. 한번은 내가 그곳이 가스실이 아니냐고 물었더니, 그자들은 낄낄대며 날더러 제법 웃기는 소리까지 해대는 여유도 아직 남아 있는 모양이라고 하더군요. 참 한심한 사람들이라는 생각이 들더군요. 도대체가 난 아예 숨쉬기조차 거북해서 입술을 앙 다문 채 콧구멍, 귓구멍은 물론이고 하다못해 온몸 살갗의 털구멍조차도 깡그리 틀어막아 버리고 싶을 지경이었는데도 말입니다.

그런데 여길 오니까 훨씬 숨을 내쉬기가 편해졌어요. 후우, 후우. 이걸 좀 보세요. 목구멍으로 공기가 드나드는

ber, and they snickered, saying I must still have the wherewithal to crack a pretty good joke. I thought what pitiful beings they were. I mean there I was, having so much trouble breathing and I pursed my lips and felt like closing off my nostrils and ears and plugging up every pore on my skin.

But now that I'm here, it's been so much easier to breathe. Hooo, hooo, see that? Doesn't it sound much smoother, the way the air is passing through my throat? Ooh, I really feel as though I escaped from the poison gas for the first time in a long while. Doctor, your face looks nice and full, with a good healthy complexion, probably because you breathe this less-polluted air every day. I wish I could somehow have the good luck to stay in this hospital for a long time. Shoot. That would not be likely, right? No way they would let me go so easy... those sons of bitches. By the way, Doctor, for patients under custody like me (heh, a patient, they call me), how long is a typical stay at the hospital? I'd rather be here one more day, one more hour even, if I could avoid seeing their dammed mugs again.

At any rate, now that I think about it, I don't really want to regret how I got to come here. Thanks to

감촉이 훨씬 부드럽지 않습니까. 아아 정말 오랜만에 독가스로부터 벗어 나온 느낌이군요. 선생님께선 얼굴에 부옇게 살이 오르고 혈색도 좋아 보이시는데 아마 이렇게 덜 오염된 공기를 매일 마시는 덕분일 겁니다. 나도 어떻게 운 좋게 이 병원에서라도 오래 머물러 있게 되었으면 더 나을 텐데. 쯧. 아마 어렵겠지요? 저자들이 날 쉽게 놓아주지 않으려 할 게 뻔하니까…… 빌어먹을 자식들. 그런데 선생님. 나 같은 감호 환자의 경우엔 (으흣. 날더러 환자라구?) 대개 얼마 동안이나 병원에 있게 됩니까? 또다시 그자들의 상관대기를 보느니, 여기서 하루, 아니 한 시간이라도 더 있게 된다면 좋겠습니다만.

뭐 어쨌든, 지금에야 생각하니까 여기까지 오게 된 걸 별로 후회하고 싶지는 않습니다. 덕분에 오랜만에 차를 타고 바깥 구경도 했고…… 물론 거기서 (그 가스실 말입니다) 지냈던 게 사나흘쯤 됩니다만, 나로서는 십 년 만큼이나 지루하고 고통스러웠어요. 아까 시내에서 남평까지 오는 동안 난 줄곧 창밖만 보았지요. 차창 너머로 얼핏 드들강을 봤는데, 강물이 많이 말랐습디다. 도로변 야산의 나무들도 단풍이 약간씩 들기 시작하고 벌써 이른 벼를 베는 논도 보이더구만요. 이전에는 멋모르고 맹맹하게 지나

that, I mean, I rode in a car and got to see the outside, for the first time in ages... Of course I only spent three or four days there—in that gas chamber—but to me it was as boring and painful as ten years. On the way from downtown to Nampyeong, I kept looking outside the window. I caught a glimpse of Deudeul River through the window, and boy had it gotten dry. Leaves are beginning to change colors on the hills by the roads, and I even saw some paddies where early rice harvest was going on. I used to pass by these things without giving them a second thought, but everything suddenly looked different today. Passing the railroad crossing in Baegun-dong, where I'd go all the time, felt weird, and my eyes welled up. Folks were still walking on the familiar streets, and the old shoe repairman was sitting in his usual spot by the flowerbed near the crossing today as always. I figured not much has changed in the world in the last few days, a thought that made me feel a bit relieved. When you get down to it, I'm just an ordinary little guy, with no dreams. I've always thought to myself that I wouldn't mind it, if I had a home with a warm bed, a sweet-natured wife, and a couple of kids (Heh, we don't have any yet. We got

치곤 했는데 그 모든 것들이 오늘은 별안간 전혀 달라 보입디다. 내가 늘 다니던 백운동 철도 건널목을 지날 때는 괜히 눈물이 핑 돌고 기분이 이상했지요. 낯익은 거리로 여전히 행인들이 오가고, 언제나처럼 건널목 화단 옆에 구두를 깁는 영감이 오늘도 그 자리에 나와 앉은 걸 보니 그래도 아직 세상은 며칠 전이나 별 달라짐 없이 남아 있나 보구나 싶어지고. 그래서 조금은 맘이 놓이는 기분이었습니다. 사실 나는 어찌 보면 꿈도 없이 평범하고 시시한 녀석이거든요. 난 그저 겨울에도 불기가 잘 드는 아랫목이 있는 집 한 채에다가 심성이 유순한 아내. 그리고 아이는 둘만 (으핫. 물론 우린 아직 아이가 하나도 없지요. 늦게 결혼하기도 했고 또…… 하지만 한 달 남짓 후엔 아이가 생기죠. 아내를 닮았으면 눈이 크고 예쁜 아이일 겁니다) 낳아서 탈 없이 그럭저럭 살아갈 수 있다면 그리 억울한 느낌이 들지 않으리라고 늘 혼자 여겨왔으니까요. 생각해보세요. 난 지금껏 다른 사람들하고 똑같이 평범하고 소박한 생활을 해왔습니다. 그야말로 약하고 힘없는 소시민 그대로지요. 게다가 보시다시피 겨우 오십 킬로그램 근처에서 체중기 바늘이 왔다 갔다 하는 타고난 약골인 데다가 아직껏 닭한 마리도 목 비틀어 죽여본 적 없는 겁쟁입니다. 그런데

married late and... but we're due in about a month. If it takes after my wife, it will be a pretty kid with big eyes) and lived a relatively trouble-free life. Think about it. I have so far led an ordinary, humble life just like all other average folks. I'm the definition of a meek and feeble average Joe. Besides, I'm a born weakling, barely weighing 110 pounds soaking wet, and a scaredy cat who has never even killed a chicken by twisting its neck. But geesh, they were pressing me to confess what kind of underhanded plot I had. Confess. You know, confess. Confess? Conspiracy? Confess? Intrigue...? It was all because of that damned poison gas, you know. But what did they expect me to do? I couldn't breathe to begin with. If I relaxed just a little bit, that foul gas crept in through my nose, ears, throat, and so on, and I felt I was going to suffocate.

1. Personal Data for the Subject under Evaluation

Name: Heo, Sang-gu

Sex: Male

Age: 40

Resident Registration No.: 440518-155XXXX

Permanent Address: Dongbok-myeon, Hwasun-

도 세상에 원, 그자들은 날더러 무슨 꿍꿍이속이 있느냐
며 자백을 하라는 겁니다. 자백. 자백 말입니다. 자백·음
모·자백·모의…… 그 모든 게 바로 그 빌어먹을 독가스
때문이지 뭡니까. 하지만 날더러 대체 어쩌라는 얘깁니
까. 애초에 숨 쉴 수가 없는 걸, 잠시 틈만 보여도 콧구
멍·귓구멍·목구멍 할 것 없이 그 지독한 가스가 스멀스멀
기어들어 와 질식해버릴 것만 같다구요.

1 피감정인의 인적사항

성명: 허상구

성별: 남

나이: 40세

주민등록번호: 440518-155××××

본적: 전남 화순군 동복면

주거: 전남 광주시 화정동 8×0

직업 말씀입니까. 전 미술을 전공합니다. 좀 더 정확하
게는 만화가라고 불러야 옳을 겁니다. 어떤 사람들은 그
것도 예술에 포함시킬 수가 있겠느냐고 비아냥거리는 투
로 묻기도 하지만, 천만에요. 그 누구 앞에서라도 당당하

gun, Jeollanam-do Province

Home Address: 8X0 Hwajeong-dong, Gwangju City, Jeollanam-do Province

My occupation? I specialize in fine arts. More precisely, I should say, cartoonist. Some people ask in a snide way how that could be considered art, but absolutely. I have quite a bit of pride in my occupation so I can hold my head up high in front of anyone. They like to say painting is a static type of art expressed within a fixed and limited space, but cartoons are the exact opposite. A cartoon is made up of lines, and those lines are moving objects that vividly express the motions of living objects. Therefore, lines in cartoons always stay taut and tense like a fully stretched rubber band in order to capture varied and dynamic rhythms of a single moment. In other words, they are kind of like the tendons of a short-distance runner standing precariously at the starting line and waiting for the signal, with all the nerves in his body focused on one thing. They are most definitely not static or fixed; you could say they were the life force itself, bursting with the explosive energy that is instantaneous and breathless.

게 난 내 직업에 관한 한 충분한 자부심을 지니고 있지요. 흔히들 회화란 고정되고 제한된 공간 위에 표현되는 정지된 예술 형태라고 나불거려대지만 만화는 결코 그렇지 않다구요. 만화는 선으로 이루어지고, 그 선은 곧 살아 있는 생명체의 움직임을 생생하게 표출해내는 또 하나의 운동쳅니다. 그러므로 만화의 선은 다양하고 역동적인 한 순간의 율동을 포착하기 위해 항상 잔뜩 당겨진 고무줄처럼 팽팽하게 긴장되어 있지요. 이를테면, 신호를 기다리면서 전신의 신경을 오직 한곳으로만 집중시킨 채 아슬아슬하게 출발점 위에 서 있는 단거리 주자의 근육 힘줄과도 같다고 할까요. 그것은 결코 정지하지도 고정되어 있지도 않은, 찰나의 숨 가쁜 폭발력으로 터질 듯 충일된 생명력 그 자체라고 할 수 있습니다.

난 지금까지 (아니, 정확히 지난봄까지) 꼬박 삼 년 동안 줄곧 이 지방 H신문의 만화를 맡아서 그려왔지요. 아, 알고 계시구면요. 그래요. 맞았습니다. 그 신문의 만화와 시사만평란은 주욱 제가 그렸답니다. 흔히 그러더구면요. 요새 사람들이 신문을 손에 들고 맨 먼저 들여다보는 게 바로 만화라구요. 까닭에 신문사 측에서는 지나칠 정도로 예민한 관심을 두게 마련이고, 독자나 회사 양쪽의 기대

For three years now—no, to be precise, until this past spring—I drew the cartoons for the local H paper. Oh, you know it. Yes, that's right. I did the daily strip and the illustrations for the editorials. They like to say that the first thing readers check out when they open up a newspaper is the cartoons. Because of that, the management is overly conscious of it, and as expectations of both the reader and the paper increase, so does the sense of responsibility and duty for the cartoonist. At any rate, I always tended to be pretty satisfied with my work. I majored in Western painting for my four years in college, and after my military duty, I had a studio across from the old City Hall in Geum-dong, where I taught secondary school students for six or seven years. But more than anything, I was able to confirm to myself that I was a cartoonist only when I had a corner of a newspaper all to myself and saw those beings I created come alive and move about. And I would sometimes feel rewarded or proud because of that, albeit very, very infrequently.

But you know, Doctor. At some point I started to be afraid of sitting at the desk with a pen in my hand all of a sudden. (When did that start—oh, right. It was around the time when that atrocious

치가 크면 클수록 만화가의 책임이랄까 의무도 무겁고 힘겨워지는 게 사실이지요. 어쨌건 난 내가 하는 일에 언제나 만족하는 편이었습니다. 대학 사 년 동안 서양화를 전공했고, 제대 후에도 육칠 년가량 금동구시청 앞에서 학생들 대상으로 화실을 해본 적도 있었지만, 무엇보다도 나는 신문 한 귀퉁이를 온전히 내 몫으로 차지하고, 내가 빚어낸 인물들이 살아 움직이는 모습을 대할 때에야 비로소 스스로 만화가라는 직업을 가지고 있다는 사실을 확인할 수 있었고, 또 그래서 가끔은 보람이랄까 자부심을 느낀 적도 있었죠. 물론 그건 드물게 아주 드물게였을 뿐입니다만.

그런데 말입니다, 선생님. 언제부터인가 난 별안간 펜을 쥐고 책상 앞에 앉는 일이 점점 두려워지기 시작했습니다. (그게 언제부터였을까…… 아아, 그래. 그 끔찍스런 독가스 냄새가 사방에 폭죽처럼 터뜨려져서 건물과 집들의 지붕, 골목과 골목, 거리와 거리로 어디에나 온통 자욱하게 출렁출렁 흘러 다니기 시작했던 바로 그 무렵부터였어……)

2 감정 방법

감정받은 당일(1984. 10. ×)부터 1984. 10. ×까지 전

smell of poison gas exploded everywhere like fire-crackers and began to fill everywhere, surging and flowing over roofs of buildings and houses, alleys, and streets...)

2. Method of Evaluation

Admitted on the date of the evaluation (October XX, 1984) and kept through October XX at the M National Psychiatric Hospital located in O-myeon, M-gun, Jeollanam-do Province; this evaluation was prepared by consulting documents including: psychiatric evaluation and interview; neurological examination; physiochemical examination; electroencephalography, cranial and thoracic radiography; psychological examination including an I.Q, test; interviews with people for references; inpatient medical records; documents provided by the K City police department.

I was sitting at my desk at work one morning when the managing editor called me. I think he was coming from an editorial conference. Without warning, he glared at me, asking if I was out of my mind. The sheet with the four-panel strip I'd handed in the day before was on his desk, and we had

남 M군 O면 소재 국립 M정신병원에 입원시켜, 정신의학적 진찰 및 면담, 신경학적 검사, 이화학적 검사, 뇌파 검사, 두개골 및 흉부방사선 검사, 지능 검사를 포함한 심리 검사, 참고인과의 면담, 입원 기간 중의 병상 일지, K시 경찰서에서 제공된 서류 등을 참고하여 본 감정서를 작성하였음······

　어느 날 아침이었습니다. 언제나처럼 출근해서 책상을 마주하고 앉아 있으려니 국장이 나를 부르더군요. 편집회의를 끝내고 나온 눈치였습니다. 국장은 다짜고짜 지금 제정신이냐고 눈을 홉떠 쳐다보더군요. 책상 위엔 그 전날 내가 완성해서 넘긴 사 단짜리 만화 원고가 놓여 있었는데 그건 이미 몇 시간 전에 인쇄되어 배포해버린 것이었지요. 국장은 그것을 갈퀴같이 구부린 손가락으로 쿡쿡 찌르면서 인상을 긋고 있었습니다. 뭔가 일이 생겼구나를 직감했지만, 난 그다지 놀라지 않았지요. 어쩌면 그런 일이 조만간 닥쳐오리라고 짐작하고 있었던 까닭인지도 모르지요. "아니 여보쇼. 이번에도 누구 죽는 꼴을 또 봐야겠나? 도대체 지금 온전한 정신으로 하는 짓이요, 뭐요. 당신이 무슨 피카소야? 하다못해 당대 한국 최고의 거물

already pressed and distributed the day's paper a few hours earlier. The editor was jabbing at it with his bent finger with a scowl on his face. I intuitively knew something had happened, but I wasn't really surprised. Perhaps I had been anticipating it all along. "Look here, do you want to do me in again? Are you in your right mind, or what? Are you Picasso? Or at least a top dog in contemporary Korea? What are you doing? Do you want to screw me up and totally ruin my life? How can you, at a time like this, put this in and call it a comic strip, huh?" Unable to control his temper, the editor picked up the sheet and threw it at me, and oddly enough the paper suddenly changed to a thin and sharp razor blade and flew straight at me, hitting me squarely on the nose. The people in the office started to chuckle at once, and I couldn't help but just stand there for a while, confined by their laughter. (The sound of laughter. In the middle of their chuckling laughter, I felt as though I were listening to guns going off. Laughter, gunshots, laughs... the sound of countless guns going off indiscriminately and without interruption. Then the laughs, again.)

"If there's trouble because of this, you take care of it yourself from now on. I've got nothing to do with

쯤이나 된단 말요? 이거 왜 이러슈. 누구 망하고 신세 조지는 꼬라지를 꼭 봐야겠소? 지금이 언제라고 겁도 없이 이런 걸 만화라고 떡 그려 넣었느냔 말이요. 응." 국장은 분을 못 이기는 듯 원고를 집어 들더니 나를 향해 휙 던졌는데, 묘하게도 그것은 종이가 아니라 별안간 딱딱하면서도 날카로운 면도날로 변해버린 듯 곧장 날아와 내 콧잔등에 딱 하고 부딪히는 거였습니다. 주위의 동료들이 일제히 낄낄대기 시작하고, 그 요란한 웃음소리에 갇혀서 나는 한동안 그 자리에 우두커니 서 있을 수밖에 없었습니다. (웃음소리. 낄낄대는 그들의 웃음 속에서 나는 총성을 듣고 있는 느낌이었어. 웃음소리. 총소리. 웃음…… 숱한 총구로부터 무차별로 쏟아져 나오는 쇠콩알의 발사음. 그리고 다시 웃음소리.)

"이것 때문에 문제가 생기더라도 이젠 당신 혼자 알아서 하슈. 난 책임이 없으니까. 거, 제발 혼자만 양심가인 척하지 말라구요." 국장이 씨부렁거리는 소리를 나는 꿈속처럼 귓전으로 아스라이 듣고 있었습니다. 분노라든가 모욕감 따위의 느낌조차도 없더군요. 난 다만 눈앞에 저만치 닫힌 유리창을 깨부수고 오 층 저 아래 땅바닥으로 펄쩍 뛰어내려 버리고 싶다는 생각만 하고 있었지요. 아

it. Please, stop act like you're the only person with a conscience." I was hearing his grousing faintly as in a dream. I didn't even feel enraged or denigrated. All I kept thinking was how I wanted to break through the window and leap out onto the ground five stories below. Actually, how, instead of plummeting toward the earth the moment I took my feet off the ledge, my body might float up in the air, get out of the urban sky, and eternally float away like a balloon.

The next morning two strange men came to see me. As I tidied up what I was doing and got going with them, all my coworkers kept glancing at me with a look of apprehension in their eyes. A black car was waiting by the door. I smoked continuously during the ride. Once, when the guy sitting next to me held up his lighter, I bent forward and found that my fingers were shaking so much it was downright embarrassing. Sir, don't be nervous, it's nothing serious, said the guy, almost in a whisper and with a grin. And he actually had a pretty honest face.

The first room I went into was pretty spacious, with high ceilings. Peculiarly, the four walls were plastered white without any posters or other decora-

니, 유리창 끝에서 발을 떼는 순간, 어쩌면 내 몸뚱이는 땅을 향하고 곤두박질을 치는 게 아니라 허공으로 둥실 떠올라 이 도시의 하늘을 시원스레 벗어나서 어디론가 한없이 풍선처럼 둥둥 떠갈 수 있을지도 모른다는 생각 말이죠.

이튿날 아침나절에 웬 낯선 사내 둘이 나를 찾아왔더군요. 하던 일을 대강 챙겨놓고 그자들을 따라 나설 때까지 동료들은 모두 줄곧 불안에 찬 시선으로 흘금흘금 나를 살피고 있더군요. 현관 앞에 검은색 승용차가 기다리고 있었지요. 차 안에서 나는 연거푸 담배만 피워댔습니다. 한번은 곁의 사내가 라이터를 켜주었는데, 불을 붙이기 위해 고개를 가까이 숙이려다 보니 내 손가락이 민망스러울 만큼 후들후들 떨리고 있더군요. 선생, 너무 긴장하지 마슈. 별게 아니니까. 사내가 속삭이듯 하며 싱긋 웃더군요. 의외로 그자의 얼굴은 선량해 보입디다.

내가 처음 들어간 곳은 꽤 넓고 천장이 무척 높아 보이는 방이었지요. 기이하게도 사면을 온통 하얗게 회칠을 해놓았는데 벽엔 무슨 장식물이라든가 포스터 따위 하나도 붙어 있지 않아서 얼핏 텅 빈 공간 속에 걸어 들어와 있는 느낌이 들더구만요. 그들은 나 혼자만 남겨놓고 방

tions on them, so it kind of felt like walking into emptiness. They left me alone in the room. The only things I could look at in that totally soundless room were a blinding light bulb on the ceiling and the four walls completely plastered white. Figuring someone would show up soon, I sat in a little wooden chair in the center of the room. But no one came in for some reason. Time went by, my lips felt dried and scorched, and all I could do was crouch down in that wooden chair, its edges worn out and shiny, while being tormented by all kinds of terrible imagination and delusions. Finally, a man showed up with a tray of rice in soup and yellow radish kimchi. When he was about to turn around after putting it on the desk, I asked him what was going on. "Wait here. The person in charge isn't back yet. You'll get done soon." He replied casually and left the room. I checked my watch and it was past lunchtime. I picked up the spoon but put it down after a couple of bites because I felt as though I had sand in my mouth. I waited for several more hours once the soup got cold and white lumps of fat gathered on its cooled surface, but there was no news.

I realized it was dinnertime only when they brought in my second meal. This time I couldn't

을 나갔습니다. 아무 소리도 들리지 않는 그 방 안에서 내가 눈길을 줄 수 있는 것이라곤 다만 천장에 붙은 휘황한 전등 하나와 온통 흰색으로 칠한 네 개의 벽뿐이었지요. 누군가 다시 나타나리라고 여기며 방 중앙에 놓인 작은 나무 의자에 앉았습니다. 한데, 어찌된 셈인지 좀처럼 아무도 문을 열고 들어오지 않는 겁니다. 시간은 가고 입술은 바직바직 타들어 가는 듯 쓰고, 난 온갖 두려움에 찬 상상과 끔찍스럽기 그지없는 망상에 시달리며 어쩔 수 없이 그 모서리가 낡고 닳아서 윤기가 도는 나무 의자에 구부정하니 쭈그려 앉아 있어야만 했어요. 드디어 웬 사내가 쟁반에 국밥과 노란 무김치를 받쳐 들고 나타나더군요. 그자가 그걸 책상 위에 내려놓고 돌아서려 할 때, 난 어떻게 된 일이냐고 물었지요. "기다려보시오. 아직 담당자가 돌아오지 않았으니까. 조금 있으면 모두 끝날 거요." 사내는 천연덕스런 얼굴로 대답하고는 방을 나가버렸습니다. 시계를 보니 어느새 점심시간이 넘어 있더구만요. 수저를 들고 억지로 두어 번 뜨고 나니 입맛이 모래를 씹은 듯 떫어서 그만뒀지요. 국밥이 다 식고, 그 식어빠진 국건데기 위에 허옇게 기름이 엉겨 붙은 다음에도 또 몇 시간이 지났지만 역시 감감무소식이었습니다.

even pick up the spoon. My lips were chapped white and my tongue was burning like it had been pickled in salt. For no reason, I felt nauseated to the point where I wanted to throw up all the filth in my stomach, and my head was swimming from dizziness. More time passed, and still nobody. I was barely managing to drape myself over the chair so that I wouldn't keel over, and trying my hardest not to lose consciousness, when the door opened as in a dream and a man entered. I was already so exhausted that I was not even able to stand up when I saw him. The man was short with a stocky build. He grinned deviously to himself. "Oh, I apologize for making you wait so long. There must have been a mix-up. It's nothing serious. I sincerely apologize but I'm sure you'll understand. You may go home now. Haha." I almost let go of the chair and fell over. His senselessly loud and lively laugh was ringing in my head with its sharp metallic sound. When he saw me going blank and staying down for a while, he took out a cigarette, put it in my mouth, and kindly lit it as well. You must be tired. That's why we wanted you to eat. I take it you're like the other artists; you people don't look after your bodies. I'd say you're not good at impulse control. I

두 번째로 밥이 들어왔을 때에야 비로소 저녁때라는 걸 깨달았지요. 이번엔 아예 수저도 들지 못했습니다. 입술이 하얗게 타고 혓바닥이 소금에 절인 듯 쓰라리고 아팠습니다. 까닭 없이 배 속의 오물을 모조리 토해버리고 싶도록 속이 메스껍고, 현기증으로 머리가 어찔어찔해왔죠. 그리고 다시 얼마나 시간이 흘렀지만 여전히 아무도 나타나지 않더군요. 쓰러지지 않을 정도로만 간신히 몸을 의자에 걸쳐놓은 채 가물가물해오는 정신을 잡으려 애를 쓰는데, 문득 꿈속에서처럼 방문이 열리고 한 사내가 들어왔습니다. 이미 지칠 대로 지쳐 있어서 그자를 보고도 자리에서 일어날 수가 없었지요. 키가 작고 가슴이 딱 벌어진 단단한 체구의 사내였습니다. 그자는 음흉스레 혼자 싱긋 웃더군요. "이거, 오래 기다리게 해서 죄송합니다. 뭔가 착오가 생겼던 모양이오. 별다른 것도 아녔는데. 퍽 미안스럽습니다만 이해해주시리라 믿소. 이제 그만 댁으로 돌아가셔도 좋습니다. 허헛." 나는 하마터면 손을 놓고 의자 밑으로 굴러 떨어질 뻔했습니다. 사내의 턱없이 크고 활달한 웃음소리가 머릿속에서 날카로운 쇳소리로 쨍강 쨍강 울려대는 것 같더군요. 한동안 멍청해져서 주저앉아 있으려니, 그자가 담배를 꺼내 내 입에 물려주고 친

mean fervor and spiritedness are all good, but isn't living in this world kind of like crossing a broad street with heavy traffic? If you don't look left and right, front and back, you can get into an accident before you know it. Am I right? Hahah." Breaking into laughter, he put down on the desk what he had been holding in his hand inconspicuously, as if to say he had almost forgotten about it. At first glance it looked like an ordinary notebook, but I realized as the man started to turn its pages that it was a scrapbook of my work. "Count me as one of your fans who's long been reading your works with interest. They're fun and, how should I put it, I love the places that show a sharp wit. I've always wanted to meet you, and now that I'm seeing you in person, you look much quieter and gentler than I imagined. Except that you don't look too... healthy. Hahah."

I stood up with him. I reeled from the feeling of futility, with my legs shaky and my entire body sluggish. As I was walking out of that empty, white, square-shaped room, the man turned around, gave my shoulder a friendly grab, and looked straight into my eyes. "By the way, Sir, you might want to think a bit more as you draw from now on. Hahah.

절하게도 불까지 붙여주었습니다. "피곤하신 모양이구먼
요. 그러기에 식사는 하시라니까. 선생께서도 그렇지만,
예술가들은 대개 몸을 아끼지 않는 타입들인가 봅디다.
충동을 잘 조절할 줄 모른달까. 열정도 좋고 기백도 좋지
만 그래도 사람이 세상을 살아간다는 게 마치 번잡한 한
길을 건너는 일이나 매양 한가지가 아닙니까. 앞뒤 좌우
를 잘 살피지 않으면 신상에 사고 내기 십상이지요. 안 그
렇소, 허헛." 사내는 웃음을 터뜨리며, 문득 잊고 있었다
는 듯이 손에 들고 있던 것을 책상 위에 슬몃 펴놓더군요.
얼핏 보기엔 평범한 잡기장 같았는데, 사내가 겉장을 펼
치자 난 그것이 바로 내 만화를 오려 붙인 스크랩북이란
걸 깨달았지요. "나도 선생의 만화를 전부터 흥미 있게 읽
고 있는 애독자 가운데 한 사람이올시다. 재미있고 뭐랄
까 재치가 번뜩이는 대목이 아주 좋아요. 한번 꼭 뵙고 싶
었는데, 막상 이렇게 만나고 보니 생각보다는 훨씬 조용
하시고 부드러운 인상이시구만요. 한 가지, 건강이
좀…… 좋지 않아 뵌다는 점을 빼고는 말이죠. 하핫."

　난 사내를 따라 일어섰습니다. 다리가 후들거리고 전신
의 맥이 모조리 풀려 내리는 허탈감에 허둥거렸습니다.
그 텅 빈 사각형의 하얀 방을 나서려는데 사내가 돌아서

Please don't get the wrong idea or anything... Oh, is Heo Seong-su your father's brother?" His eyes, now focused menacingly at my face, were thin and small like fishhooks, their irises barely showing. Yet I couldn't look away, caught on the sharp points of the fishhooks. Hearing my uncle's full name sprung from the lips of that man was such an unexpected shock that I could hardly breathe for a while. I had long forgotten that name. It was a name that everyone in my extended family refrained from mentioning, one that had long passed into oblivion like a forgotten nightmare. The moment the man uttered the name of my uncle who had caused the deaths of many villagers and whose whereabouts were still unknown since he'd fled overnight to some place in Jiri Mountain, it was all I could do to keep myself from falling to my knees. He quickly held up my arm. "You have a delicate constitution. You'd better go home early and get some rest." The man whispered with a curious smile. Outside the white room was a hallway, where I left him. The man didn't say one more word. I staggered along the long hallway by myself. Clip, clip, clip... Startled by the sound of my own footsteps, I kept looking back. An indiscernible fear caused by all kinds of suspicions kept

며 어깨를 다정스레 잡더니 내 눈을 정면으로 들여다보는 거였지요. "그런데 선생. 거, 앞으로는 잘 좀 생각해가면서 그려야겠습디다. 하핫. 뭐 그렇다고 오해는 마시고…… 참, 허성수 씨가 선생의 큰아버님 되시던가?" 나를 쏘아보는 그자의 매서운 두 눈은 낚싯바늘처럼 아주 가늘고 작아서 이쪽에선 눈동자가 거의 보이지 않을 정도였지요. 하지만 난 그 낚싯바늘의 뾰죽한 끝에 걸려 시선을 옴짝달싹할 수가 없었습니다. 그자의 입에서 큰아버지의 이름 석 자가 불쑥 튀쳐나왔다는 사실이 너무나 놀랍고 충격적이어서 한동안 숨을 내쉬기가 어려웠어요. 난 벌써 오래전에 그 이름을 까맣게 잊고 있었습니다. 나뿐만 아니라 우리 식구들과 일가친척들 간에는 이미 들먹이기를 꺼려하는, 그래서 어느덧 흉흉한 꿈 얘기처럼 아득하게 망각되어버린 이름이었으니까요. 마을 사람들 목숨 여럿을 끊어놓은 채 지리산 어딘가로 야밤에 흔적도 없이 도망쳐 버린 뒤로는 아직까지 생사를 모르고 있는 큰아버지의 이름을 사내에게서 듣는 순간, 나는 하마터면 그자 앞에 무릎을 꺾고 주저앉을 뻔했지요. 재빨리 부축을 해주더군요. 몸이 허약하시구면, 일찍 들어가서서 쉬시는 게 좋겠소. 사내가 묘한 웃음을 흘리며 속삭였습니다. 그

clutching at my neck. That I was not alone now; that I wasn't the only one walking the hallway; that I might never again be alone and free; that someone was secretly tailing me...

It was raining outside. I was amazed that it was already nighttime. I checked my watch to find it was after ten. Yes, twelve hours. I had spent half of a full day in that white room, staring at those four white walls, nothing but white like funeral clothing. You know the old tale of how this one guy took a deep nap in the middle of chopping wood in the mountains, and when he woke up, decades had passed? That's how I felt at first. Like a prisoner who had been released after a long confinement within brick walls, things that had just happened seemed far, far away and thoroughly unreal. Even after I was well out of that building, I was dumbfounded and everything felt unfamiliar.

I started to walk in the rain. It was truly pouring down, the kind you don't get often. The wind would gust, making it rain sideways. I only took a few steps before I was soaked through, with water dripping from my underwear. But I kept tottering on, getting pounded by thick raindrops like a demented man, without thinking to buy an umbrel-

하얀 방을 나오니 복도가 나타났고, 거기서 사내와 헤어졌지요. 사내는 끝내 그 이상의 말은 하지 않더군요. 난 비칠대며 길다란 복도로 홀로 걸어 나왔습니다. 뚜벅, 뚜벅, 뚜벅…… 몇 번이나 내 발소리에 놀라 흠칫 뒤를 돌아다보곤 했는지 몰라요. 지금 난 혼자가 아닐 거라는 생각, 혼자서만 이 복도를 걸어가고 있는 것이 아니리라는 생각, 앞으로는 어쩌면 영영 홀로 자유로울 수 없게 되고 말았을 거라는 생각, 누군가가 소리 없이 숨어 나를 뒤밟아 오고 있을 거라는 생각…… 그런 온갖 의혹이 형언키 어려운 두려움으로 목덜미를 자꾸만 나꿔채곤 했습니다.

밖은 비가 오고 있더군요. 어느새 밤이 되어 있다는 사실에 놀랐습니다. 시계를 보니 열 시가 넘은 시각이었습니다. 열두 시간. 그래요. 난 꼬박 하루의 반을 그 하얀 방 안에서 다만 그 수의처럼 하얗고 하얗기만 한 네 개의 벽을 바라보며 보냈던 것입니다. 그런 옛날 얘기 아시죠. 산에서 나무를 하다가 낮잠 한숨 늘어지게 자고 일어났더니 그동안에 몇십 년이 흘러가 버렸더라는. 정말 처음엔 그런 지경을 당한 것만 같았어요. 마치 오랫동안 벽돌담 안에 갇혀 있다가 갓 풀려 나온 죄수처럼 바로 조금 전까지의 일들이 아득히 멀게 여겨지고 전혀 현실감이 느껴지지

la. I didn't even know where I was headed. The cold streaks of rain were rather refreshing. I wished that I could just disappear somewhere right then, that I could evaporate from this world like steam, without leaving a trace. With severe rain late in the evening, most stores were closed, and there were few passersby on the streets. If you take a left at the end of Chungjang-ro 1-ga, you get to the square in front of the governor's office. With my body completely drenched, I began to walk along the path around the square. For some reason, I just kept roaming around Geumnam-ro, even as I knew I should hail a cab and go home before anything. I crouched down on the front steps of the NFFC (National Federation of Fisheries Cooperative) building to get out of the rain for a bit. I checked my pockets for a cigarette, but everything was soggy so I just threw them out. Stretched in front of me was the desolate square, save for an occasional automobile scooting around the water fountain, and eerily without anyone on foot.

I don't know how long I stayed put, crouched on the steps. I may even have dozed off a couple of times looking like a mouse doused in rain. The electronic clock above the governor's office across

않았으니까요. 그 건물을 완전히 빠져나온 후에도 한참은 여전히 어리벙벙하고 눈에 뵈는 것들이 생소하기만 했습니다.

빗속을 걷기 시작했습니다. 억수같이 쏟아지는 참 드물게 보는 대단한 비였지요. 간간이 불어치는 세찬 바람에 빗살이 비스듬히 비껴 날리곤 했습니다. 채 몇 걸음 옮겨 놓기도 전에 전신이 흠뻑 젖어버려서 내의 밑까지 빗물이 줄줄 흘러내릴 지경이었습니다. 하지만 우산을 사야겠다는 생각도 없이 난 그냥 정신 나간 사람처럼 억센 장대비를 맨몸으로 두들겨 맞으며 허청허청 걸었지요. 어디로 가리라는 작정도 없이 무턱대고 말입니다. 차가운 빗줄기가 차라리 후련했어요. 이대로 어디로든 홀홀 사라져버렸으면, 수증기처럼 흔적도 남기지 않고 이 지상으로부터 증발해버리고 말았으면, 하고 난 소망했습니다. 늦은 시각에 비까지 쏟아져 내리는 탓인지 상가는 대부분 닫혀 있었고 오가는 사람들도 퍽 뜸했습니다. 충장로 일가를 벗어나서 왼쪽으로 꺾어지면 도청 앞 광장이 나옵니다. 온몸이 엉망으로 젖은 채 난 광장을 끼고 도는 길을 따라 걷기 시작했지요. 무엇보다 차를 잡아타고 집으로 돌아가야 하리라는 생각을 하면서도 왠지 난 그저 금남로 주변

the street was nearing midnight, and the rain kept blurring the light from the working half of the lamppost in front of the Military Training Facility across the street. It was right then that I had a whiff of that odor for the first time. It was a weird smell. It was as if an unidentifiable stench were rising up from somewhere close by. Honest. Trust me. You have got to believe me. There really was this odd and suspicious smell. You know what? Since whenever, that smell is always blended like syrup in any rain that falls on this city like the memory of a gigantic, long-concealed scheme and blood-red sin that gives you shudders. That's what gives the black tinge to the nasty and gloomy rain that falls on the roofs of this city all the time. Black rain. That's the rain of death. That cursed rain of sin that's as toxic as the yellow rain coming down densely on the jungles of Vietnam. You don't know? Really? That the rain darker than dark ink is pummeling us every single day of the year on our heads, faces, and bodies, everywhere, as we go about our lives? One contact with a drop of that rain, and there's a black hole on that spot right away. Hands, feet, chest, forehead, eyes, nose, neck, back, shoulders, thighs, calves, head, belly, skull... wherever, the indiscriminate and

을 이리저리 맴돌고만 있었습니다. 수협 건물 앞 계단에서 잠시 비를 피하느라 쭈그려 앉았지요. 문득 담배 생각이 나서 호주머니를 더듬어보니 이미 흥건히 젖어 있어서 땅에 버렸습니다. 눈앞으로는 횅한 광장이 보이고, 분수대를 돌아 이따금 차들이 바쁘게 달려가곤 할 뿐 행인들의 모습은 기이하리만큼 눈에 띄지 않더군요.

내가 얼마나 오래 그 계단 위에 쪼그려 앉아 있었는지 잘 모르겠어요. 영락없이 물 맞은 생쥐 꼴로 잠깐씩 졸았었는지도 모르죠. 맞은편 도청 옥상의 전광 시계판이 자정을 가리키고 있었고, 길 건너 상무관 앞 외눈박이 가로등이 빗속에서 흐릿해졌다가는 다시 시야로 떠오르곤 했습니다. 바로 그때였어요. 난 그 순간에 처음으로 그 냄새를 맡아냈던 거라구요. 기묘한 냄새였어요. 정체를 알 수 없는 고약한 냄새가 가까운 어디에선가로부터 스멀스멀 피어오르고 있는 듯했습니다 정말입니다. 믿으세요. 제 말을 믿으시라니까요. 진짜로 이상하고 수상쩍은 냄새가 난다구요. 그렇게 생각지 않으세요. 언제부터인지 모르게 이 도시 위에 내리는 빗속에는 틀림없이 그 냄새가 마치도 오래오래 감추어져 온 엄청난 음모와 소름 끼치는 핏빛 죄악의 기억처럼 눅진하게 스며들어 있다니까요. 때문

disorderly raindrops pelt down on our physical body, making big and little holes, bam, bam, bam, or sometimes leaving numerous deep and blackish tattoos on the fair skin of maidens. I'm pretty sure you know. Right? Hahahaa. Those countless holes that are deeply engraved in the minds of many people, including you and me, who are going about our lives casual on the outside, pretending not to know anything, and those various tattoos that are beautiful (yes, the more beautiful the more they are vile), blue-blackish like an animal carcass that's just begun to decompose, or reddish and blackish...

At first I thought that foul and atrocious smell had to be coming from somewhere nearby, so I stuck out my neck to look around in the darkness, but I wasn't able to come up with anything. Meanwhile that unidentifiable smell was only intensifying, rather than going away. It came to a point where I had to hold my nose, and though I tried my hardest to ascertain its source, twitching my nose, all I saw was the torrential rain and the pitch-black darkness. How shall I put it—at any rate, it was truly a disgusting and odious smell. It instantly made your throat sore and swollen and your lungs feel suffocated like they were going to burst. Then, suddenly,

에 이 도시의 지붕으로 구죽죽이 내리는 비는 언제나 시커먼 빛깔을 띠고 있지요. 검은 비. 그것은 죽음의 비예요. 베트남의 밀림 지대 위로 자욱하게 쏟아지는 황색비만큼이나 유독하기 그지없는 그 저주받은 죄악의 비, 모르세요? 정말? 우리들은 아직도 삼백육십오 일 날마다 그 먹물보다 진한 검은 비를 머리·얼굴·몸뚱이 할 것 없이 온통 두들겨 맞으며 살아가고 있다는 사실을 말입니다. 그 빗방울이 한 번 닿기만 하면 그 자리마다에는 금방 까만 구멍이 뻥뻥 뚫리게 되지요. 손, 발, 가슴, 이마, 눈, 코, 목, 등허리, 어깨, 허벅지, 장딴지, 뒤통수, 배, 두개골…… 그 어디에든 빗방울은 우리들의 육신을 노리고 무차별로 어지러이 날아와 뻥, 뻐엉, 뻥, 구멍을 뚫어놓기도 하고, 혹은 거무죽죽하고 깊숙한 문신을 고운 처녀의 살갗에 숱하게 남겨놓기도 하지요. 아마 알고 계실 겁니다. 그렇죠? 으흐흐흐훗. 겉으로는 아무것도 모르는 척 천연스레 살아가고 있는 선생님과, 나와, 그리고 다른 더 많은 사람들의 마음속에 깊이깊이 판박이되어 있는 그 무수한 구멍들이며, 또 마악 부패해가기 시작하는 짐승의 시신처럼 푸르딩딩한 듯, 혹은 불그죽죽 거무튀튀한 듯 아름다운 (그래요. 아아, 추악하기 때문에 더더욱 아름다운) 그 온갖 문신들

I knew its identity just like that. Poison gas. Yes, it was poison gas. When I was doing my military duty, we had ranger training once every year, and I remembered breathing in poison gas very similar to it. After putting gas masks on dozens of us and having us squat and wobble into a tent that had been sealed off everywhere, the drill instructors would close the door behind us and order us to take off the masks immediately. Of course they kept their masks on. You couldn't help taking off your mask if you didn't want to get beat up, and it was pure hell from there on. Merely a couple of minutes of exposure to the poison gas would keep your eyes watery and nose runny, making you suffer even after you darted outside. But curiously enough, I smelled that poison gas from the past again at that moment, when I was waiting out the rain on the front steps of the NFFC. Yes, I was right. It was poison gas, frightening and cruel, making you faint after tearing your nose apart and choking your throat. Sometimes it smells like heavily rusted metal, and other times it smells like blood from the fresh carcass of an animal, still somewhat warm... perhaps it is the scent of immense sin, or that of an ugly betrayal, passed down through generations of the human

을 말입니다……

　처음에 난 그 고약하고 끔찍스런 냄새가 분명히 가까운 어디선가에서 풍겨오는 것이리라 짐작하고는 고개를 빼어 어둠 속을 살펴보았지만 아무것도 찾아낼 수가 없었습니다. 정체 모를 그 냄새는 사라지지 않고 오히려 점점 더 또렷하게 느껴져 오는 거였지요. 마침내는 코를 쥐어 싸야 할 만큼 강렬해지기 시작했고, 난 연신 코를 벌름거리며 그것의 출처를 확인하려 애를 썼지만 보이는 것은 다만 쏟아지는 폭우와 깜깜한 어둠뿐이었습니다. 뭐랄까, 하여튼 참으로 역겹고 지긋지긋한 냄새였어요. 단번에 목구멍이 칵 막혀오고 가슴이 터질 듯 답답해올 지경이었으니까. 그러다가 불현듯 나는 그것의 정체를 짐작해냈던 것입니다. 독가스. 그렇습니다. 독가스였어요. 군대에 있을 때 해마다 한 차례씩 유격 훈련을 받는데 그때 바로 그와 비슷한 독가스를 마신 경험이 있지요. 사방을 밀폐시킨 천막 안으로 방독면을 씌운 채 오리걸음으로 수십 명을 뒤뚱뒤뚱 기어 들어가게 한 다음, 훈련 조교들이 뒤에서 문을 닫고 우리들에게 즉시 방독면을 벗으라고 명령합니다. 물론 가스로 자욱한 그 안에서 그자들은 방독면을 쓴 채로지요. 얻어터지지 않으려고 우리는 도리 없이

race since the beginning of time, hidden deep inside our blood.

I was short of breath from the smell that threatened to take my nose off. Meanwhile, the rain kept pouring down, and once in a while there was the skewed light from passing cars. I must have dozed off a bit, sitting against the closed shutter. When I woke up after I don't know how long, the rain streaks were blowing into where I was sitting. By then, the wind was blowing pretty hard as well. The square was totally vacant, and I could see by the light of the street lamps that the gingko trees on the sidewalks were toppling over at an angle, all disheveled, and then barely managing to stand up again. The electronic clock on the rooftop of the governor's office read a quarter past one. Right then, I felt a spell of fear, and chills ran through my body from the cold and hunger, my jaw trembling. I tried to get up by holding on to the wall, but my body would not cooperate. I stayed put, trying to get my bearings, while the rain kept coming down raucously and the disheveling wind was sweeping the streets insanely. Every time the rain and the wind were rolling around, entwined in each other's arms, dismal and terrifying shrieks buzzed from

방독면을 벗게 되고 그 순간부터는 아예 지옥입니다. 불과 이삼 분 동안에 거기서 들이마신 독가스 때문에 밖으로 튀어나와서도 눈물 콧물을 질질 흘려대며 고통스러워해야 합니다. 그런데 묘하게도 난 그때의 그 독가스 냄새를 그 순간, 비를 피하고 있던 수협 앞 계단에서 다시금 맡았던 거예요. 그래, 맞았어요. 콧구멍을 찢어내고 목을 졸라대어 이윽고 질식하게 만드는 무섭고 잔인한 독가스 말입니다. 때로는 녹슨 쇠붙이 내음 같기도 하고, 혹은 비릿하면서도 아직 온기가 남아 있는 짐승의 시신으로부터 솔솔 풍겨 나오는 피 내음도 같은…… 아마도 그건 까마득한 옛날부터 인간의 피 속에 숨어 내려온 엄청난 죄악의 냄새이거나 추악하기 그지없는 배신의 냄새일지도 몰라요.

난 콧구멍이 터질 듯한 그 냄새에 숨이 가빠왔습니다. 그런 순간에도 비는 억수같이 퍼붓고 있었고 이따금 스쳐 지나가는 차량의 기우뚱한 불빛이 보였지요. 그러다가 닫힌 서터문에 등을 기댄 채 깜빡 잠이 들었었나 봅니다. 얼마나 지났을까. 얼결에 눈을 떠보니 빗발이 어느 틈엔가 내가 앉아 있는 자리까지 마구 들이치고 있더군요. 이제는 대단히 거센 바람까지 불어대기 시작하고 있는 참이었

roofs of houses, from the tips of utility poles, from power lines and the streets, and from roofs of buildings and the tops of the flag poles outside government offices. Those were cries. The disconsolate wails, the shouts, and the death cries of numerous people screaming with their mouths wide open, and the sounds of chaotic footsteps of those being chased breathlessly, the sounds, the sounds... oh, it was such a nightmare. Who could imagine such a horrifying scene?

And that was the moment that I saw it. I really did see it with my own two eyes. So far, everyone I've told this to has said I was lying, that I must have hallucinated, no matter how adamant I was. But shit, it was real. I really saw it. With these two eyeballs. Clearly. Will you please believe me, Doctor...? Or, maybe those people were right. Maybe it was a mirage that I saw. Hahaha... But, you know, I just cannot believe that it was only a mirage. Because I really did see it. Honest.

It was people. I began to see countless kids and young folks, and then men and women who looked older. Right there in the middle of the square, in the pitch-black darkness. It had been a good while since the last bus of the night, yet out from the

습니다. 광장은 텅 비어 있고 가로등 불빛에 길가 은행나무들이 가지째 머리를 풀어 헤치고 비스듬히 쓰러졌다가는 가까스로 몸을 일으키곤 하는 게 보였습니다. 도청 옥상의 전광 시계가 한 시 십오 분을 가리키고 있었지요. 순간, 더럭 무서움증이 일면서 추위와 배고픔으로 전신에 한기가 들고 턱이 와들와들 떨려왔습니다. 벽을 붙잡고 일어서려 했는데 몸이 전혀 말을 들어주지 않더군요. 정신을 차리려고 한참 그 자리에 다시 주저앉아 있으려니 비는 악머구리 끓듯 쏟아져 내리고 머리채를 풀어 헤친 바람은 미친 듯 거리를 휩쓸며 돌아다니고 있었습니다. 비와 바람이 한데 엉켜 뒹굴 때마다 집집의 지붕에서, 전신주 끝에서, 전깃줄과 길바닥 위에서, 건물의 옥상과 관공서의 깃대 끝에서 음산하고 소름 끼치는 아우성 소리가 웅웅 울려 나왔지요. 그건 울음소리였어요. 수많은 사람들이 커다랗게 입을 벌리고 고래고래 질러대는 비통한 울음소리, 고함 소리, 단말마의 비명 소리, 그리고 숨넘어가도록 쫓겨가는 어지러운 발소리, 소리, 소리…… 아아, 차라리 악몽이었습니다. 그렇듯 소름 끼치는 광경을 누가 상상이나 할 수 있겠습니까……

그런데 바로 그 순간에 난 보았습니다. 분명히 이 두 눈

darkness where the rain and the wind were rolling around all entwined, something was wiggling and straightening up its body. At first it looked like a flickering shadow, then the shape became more definite bit by bit. With hushed breath and wide-open eyes, I watched those countless people rise from the asphalt one by one and stand up, straightening out their slumped bodies. From beginning to end. Tap tap tap... The rain pounded down furiously on the pavement of the square, taking off dark stains on the asphalt, old grime caught in the tiny nooks on the surface, and layers of soot from smog. After a little white, somewhere along the thick streets, it was disclosing one by one the clots of red-black stains and the countless footsteps and screams, even the final breaths of those in their waning moments, all tangled together one late spring day of that year. One, two, four, five, ten, twelve... Before I knew it, the square was being filled with thousands of shadows, and they all had a red flower petal in their mouth, every single one of them. Those petals, as big and wide as those of a lily magnolia and of a much finer and brighter shade of red, were stuck to their lips, cheeks, necks, chests, ribs and thighs. Appearing all red from the

으로 똑똑히 목격했다니까요. 지금껏 내가 아무리 애길 해도 만나는 사람마다 모두 거짓말이라고, 헛것을 본 것 이라면서 믿어주지 않았지만, 옘병할, 그건 진짜라구요. 분명히 보았단 말입니다. 이 두 눈알로요, 똑똑하게. 믿어 주시겠습니까, 선생님…… 아니, 어쩌면 그 사람들 말이 옳을지도 몰라. 난 그저 헛것을 본 것에 지나지 않는 것인 지 모르죠. 으흐흣…… 하지만 말씀예요. 그게 환영일 뿐 이라는 사실이 난 믿어지지가 않아요. 왜냐면 분명히 나 는 보았기 때문이죠. 정말이라니까요.

사람들이었어요. 수많은 아이들과 젊은이들, 그리고 더 나이가 들어 보이는 남자와 여자들의 모습이 보이기 시작 했습니다. 거기 칠흑 같은 어둠 속, 바로 그 광장 한가운 데에서 말입니다. 차량은 오래전부터 끊겨져 있었는데 비 와 바람이 서로 엉켜 뒹구는 어둠 저편으로부터 무엇인가 가 꿈틀거리며 서서히 몸을 일으켜 세우기 시작했습니다. 처음에 그것은 얼핏 무슨 그림자의 어른거림처럼 보이다 가 차츰 윤곽이 뚜렷해지더군요. 나는 숨을 죽이고 눈알 을 부릅뜬 채, 수많은 사람들이 아스팔트 바닥에서 하나 둘 구부정한 몸을 일으켜 세우는 보습을 지켜보았습니다. 처음부터 끝까지. 두두 두두 두두…… 빗줄기는 엄청난

petals covering their faces, they then began to move slowly as one. With every slow step they took, stretched in a line and roped together like a package of dried yellow croakers,[1] I could almost hear the clanks of fetters and the metal chains dragging on the ground. I urgently yelled toward them as they were headed away from me, with their backs to me, into the darkness. Hey there. where are you going? Hello? But my tongue got paralyzed and I ended up not being able to utter a sound. In the meantime, they kept walking away, and soon they completely disappeared. I must have lost consciousness at that moment. When I opened my eyes next, I was in an emergency room of a university hospital, and my wife was weeping and sniffling by my bed. I was found by passing patrolmen who carried me all the way there, she said.

After that nightmarish night, I was suddenly afraid of picking up a pen. Going to the office every morning and finishing the strip to be handed over for the day felt more and more strenuous and wearying. The act of making the first mark on a blank space of white paper now struck me as being greatly significant, and every time I faced an empty sheet, the memory of the four white walls agonized

기세로 광장의 포도 위를 두들겨대면서 아스팔트에 그려진 검은 얼룩이며 그 노면의 미세한 틈마다에 낀 해묵은 먼지와 매연에 찌든 땟국을 벗겨내고 있었지요. 이윽고는 두꺼운 길바닥 어디쯤인가에서, 그해 늦은 봄 어느 날 바로 그 자리마다에 엉겨 붙은 검붉은 얼룩과 숱한 발자국과 고함 소리, 그리고 누군가의 식어가는 마지막 숨결들까지도 하나하나 들춰내고 있었습니다. 하나, 둘, 넷, 다섯, 열, 열둘…… 어느덧 광장은 수십 수백의 그림자로 채워지기 시작했는데, 그들은 한결같이 입에 빨간 꽃잎을 하나씩 물고 있는 채로 였어요. 자목련 꽃이파리만큼이나 크고 넓적하면서도 훨씬 곱고 선연한 붉은색 꽃잎은 그들의 입술과 뺨에도, 목덜미와 가슴과 옆구리와 허벅지에도 붙어 있었습니다. 그 때문에 온통 붉게만 보이는 그들의 얼굴은 이윽고 한덩어리가 된 채 천천히 움직이기 시작했지요. 한 두름의 굴비처럼 기다랗게 꿰어진 그들이 한 줄로 길게 늘어서서 느릿느릿 걸음을 옮길 때마다 찔걱대는 차꼬 소리와 땅에 끌리는 쇠사슬 소리가 들려오는 것 같았습니다. 등을 돌리고 어둠 저편으로 멀어져 가는 그들을 향해 나는 다급하게 외쳤지요. 여보시오들. 어디로 가는 거요. 여보시오. 하지만 헛바닥이 오그라들어 끝내 아

me, along with that awful smell of poison gas. I could not breathe. I'd lose my voice just like that and my chest would feel tight as though somebody were forcefully choking my throat. Every day, my head would be swimming with the gross taste of the fatty soup, my uncle, and the frightening memories from the long and narrow hallway that went on forever with no end in sight and from the city square. More than anything, Doctor, I could not draw straight lines. Straight lines. The powerful and decisive lines which sharply and wholly separate all the things in this world in half without one iota of doubt. My hand would shake so hard holding a pen, I was unable to draw even a simple straight line without a ruler. As a result, we had to print a few issues of the newspaper without the comic strip. It is all because of the poison gas. I could never get away from that foul thing—at the office, at home, on the street, or in bed. I tried wearing a surgical mask in the middle of summer,[2] and spent a whole day covering my nose with a handkerchief, all in vain. Once, when I pleaded at a clinic, they recommended that I should have therapy with a psychiatrist. I was speechless. I mean, think about it. Why should I be the only one to suffer like this

무 소리도 내뱉지 못하고 말았습니다. 그사이 그들은 자꾸 멀어져 가더니 곧 완전히 사라져버렸습니다. 아마도 난 그때 정신을 놓아버렸었나 봅니다. 눈을 뜨니 대학 병원 응급실이었고, 아내가 침대 곁에서 훌쩍이고 있었습니다. 지나던 방범대원들이 발견하고는 거기까지 업어 왔다더군요.

악몽 같은 그날 밤 이후, 난 갑자기 펜을 잡기가 두려워지기 시작했습니다. 출근해서 그날 넘겨줄 만화를 완성해야 하는 일이 점점 고역스럽고 힘겹게 느껴졌지요. 텅 빈 백지의 공간에 최초의 한 점을 똑 떨어뜨린다는 사실이 별안간 엄청난 의미로 내게 다가왔고 그때마다 그 네 개의 하얀 벽의 기억과 함께 끔찍스런 독가스 냄새가 날 괴롭히곤 했습니다. 숨을 쉴 수가 없었지요. 목구멍이 금방 잠겨오고 흡사 누군가 내 목을 완강한 힘으로 졸라대는 듯이 가슴이 답답해지곤 하는 거예요. 느끼한 국밥의 맛과, 큰아버지와, 가도 가도 출구가 나타나지 않을 듯한 길고 좁다란 복도와 광장에서의 무서운 기억들이 날마다 뇌리를 휘저었습니다. 무엇보다도, 선생님, 난 직선을 그릴 수가 없었다구요. 직선, 세상의 모든 사물을 추호의 의심도 없이 두 쪽으로 날렵하고도 완전하게 갈라놓는 바로

from poison gas in my life, when others are apparently unaware of it entirely? How come others don't smell its foul odor? Why is that, Doctor?

I ended up quitting my job at the newspaper. No, that's incorrect. They kicked me out. One day, without warning. "Mr. Heo, you seem to be in very bad health. I'm afraid you won't be able to handle your work here anymore, so don't hate me too much, but I think you'd better recuperate at home for a while." That's what the editor said, but that's all garbage. You think I wouldn't know his black intention? Fired. Yes, I became an unemployed person. Still, when it happened, I could not make sense of it all, and I did not know how to take the fact that I'd gotten the ax. But taking the space away from a cartoonist is similar to removing the vocal cords from an opera singer. Come to think of it, that small corner of the newspaper that was my domain might have been the absolutely necessary breathing hole of my own, connecting me with the world. I realized only later that I'd started to die a little every day once that hole got clogged.

In the last six months since I quit my job, I've done very little. Mostly, I'd be holed up at home all day, lying on the heated floor, doing nothing, and

그 강력하면서도 단호한 선 말입니다. 펜을 쥔 손가락이 덜덜 떨려와서, 자가 없이는 아무리 간단한 직선이라도 영영 그려낼 수가 없어졌어요. 그 까닭에 신문은 몇 번인가 만화가 펑크 난 채 찍혀져 나가야 했습니다. 모두가 독가스 탓이죠. 회사에서나 집에서나, 거리에서도 잠자리에서도 그 지독한 놈으로부터 벗어날 수가 없었으니까요. 한여름에도 마스크를 쓰기도 하고, 온종일 손수건으로 코를 막은 채 견디기도 했으나 아무 소용이 없더군요. 한번은 병원에 찾아가 하소연을 했더니, 기관지엔 이상이 없다며 차라리 정신신경과를 찾아서 상담을 해보는 게 어떻겠느냐고 했어요. 기가 막혀서, 원, 생각해보십시오. 어째서 나 혼자만 이렇게 독가스 때문에 고통을 받고 살아야 합니까. 남들은 전혀 모르고 지낸다는데 말이죠. 왜 다른 사람들은 그 지독한 가스 냄새를 못 맡고 있지요? 그건 어째서입니까, 선생님.

결국 신문사를 그만두었습니다. 아니죠. 그건 틀린 말이군요. 그자들이 날 쫓아낸 것입니다. 어느 날 느닷없이 말예요. "허 선생, 건강이 몹시 좋지 않은 모양이구먼. 암만해도 더 이상 일을 계속하기엔 무리이겠고 하니, 너무 서운해 하지 말고 당분간 집에서 요양을 하는 것이 좋겠

not caring to know when the day ended and the night began. I went on a couple of trips, but they were insignificant and uninteresting. Watching the house after my wife left for work every morning was my routine, and it was actually the only service I could provide for her. Haha. My wife teaches in elementary school. She would rise at dawn, busily prepare the meals, then wobble out the bedroom door to get her heavy body to work, and I would see her off, still lying under the covers with sleepy eyes. She always has to hurry to catch the bus for her commute of over an hour and a half to some countryside school in Hwasun, and I take my time getting up around noon and have by myself a meal that's both breakfast and lunch. After that, I get the morning paper and peruse it a couple of times, including all the ads, or flip through old magazines and fiction books before taking an afternoon nap, and stay lying around like a log until my wife comes home and wakes me up. I have yet to feel bored or tired of such a lifestyle. For some reason, my head and neck would always be achy and tight, and I'd feel drained all over and sleepy. Still, I could not bring myself to grab a drawing pen, even to scratch a doodle-like sketch. I started to drink alone

소." 국장이 그럽디다만, 다아 웃기는 소리죠. 내가 그 검은 속셈을 모릅니까. 해고죠. 실직자가 된 거라구요. 그래도 그때엔 뭐가 뭔지, 목이 잘려진다는 사실을 어떻게 받아들여야 할지조차도 잘 모르겠더군요. 하지만 만화가에게서 지면을 빼앗는 것은 성악가의 성대를 제거해버리는 일이나 마찬가지 일입니다. 그러고 보니 내게 맡겨진 신문의 그 조그마한 공간은 아마 세상과 통한 내 자신의 최소한의 숨구멍이었는지도 모르지요. 그 숨구멍마저 막혀버리자 난 하루하루 내가 조금씩 죽어가고 있다는 사실을 뒤늦게야 깨닫기 시작했지요.

직장을 그만둔 뒤, 지난 육 개월 동안 나는 거의 아무 일도 하지 않고 지냈습니다. 종일 집안에 틀어박혀 구들장을 등지고 빈둥거리며 낮이 가는지 밤이 오는지도 모르고 누워 보내는 일이 많았지요. 어쩌다 한두 번 여행을 가본 적은 있었지만 별 흥미도 의미도 가져다주지 못했어요. 아침마다 아내가 출근하고 나면 집을 보는 일이 자연히 내 일과처럼 되어버렸고, 또 그것이 실은 내가 아내에게 베풀 수 있는 유일한 봉사인 셈이었지요. 흐흐. 아내는 국민학교에서 아이들을 가르치고 있습니다. 이른 새벽부

frequently from the despair that I might not be able to do any work ever again. I couldn't stand the thought that everything had ended, or the enormous fear that I might not be able to draw ever again. When I got drunk, I slept, and when I woke up, I drank some more... as my wife says, maybe I have become a permanent failure.

Let's see, it had to be last Sunday. Because my wife was home during the day. As always, I was in bed instead of having breakfast, but I woke up, startled by what I heard in my sleep: eerie moans from somewhere. Myeong-gi-yaah. Oh my. My poor child. The mournful voice that was at once like a cry and a melody was coming from the next room. I sat up instantly but had to lie back down. My body was soaked in cold sweat. My wife, who was sewing next to me, got alarmed in turn, asking me whether I'd had a terrible dream.

The voice with the plaintive moaning belonged to Haenam-Daek, an old woman who has been living in the little room off the entrance to our house for a long time. Though she is only in her early sixties, the many age spots on her face make her look like she is well into her seventies. Haenam-Daek had a son called Myeong-gi, about twenty-two, and I

터 일어나 분주하게 밥을 지어놓고는 무거운 몸으로 출근하기 위해 뒤뚱대며 방문을 밀고 나가는 아내의 뒷모습을 나는 늘 이불 속에서 졸린 눈으로 전송하곤 했지요. 버스로 한 시간 반이 족히 걸리는 화순 어느 시골 학교까지 가려면 아내는 언제나 서둘러야 했고, 난 열두 시가 다 되어서야 어슬렁어슬렁 일어나서 아침 겸 점심을 혼자 먹곤합니다. 그러고 나면 아침 신문을 찾아내어 광고까지 두어 번씩 샅샅이 훑거나, 묵은 잡지며 소설책 나부랭이를 뒤적이다가 다시 낮잠을 자기 시작하면 아내가 집으로 돌아와서 흔들어 깨울 때까지 줄창 통나무처럼 누워 있는 겁니다. 거의 매일같이 되풀이되는 그런 생활이 지루하다거나 따분하게 느껴진 적은 없었습니다. 웬일인지 늘상 뒷머리가 뻐근해지면서 전신이 피곤하고 졸립기만 했으니까요. 그러면서도 화필을 잡거나 하다못해 낙서 같은 스케치라도 끄적거려보지는 끝끝내 못했지요. 결국 난 아무 일도 할 수 없을 것만 같은 절망감으로 번번이 혼자 술을 마시기 시작했습니다. 모든 게 끝장이라는 생각, 더는 그림을 그릴 수 없을지도 모른다는 엄청난 두려움 때문에 견딜 수가 없었으니까요. 취하면 잠들고, 깨고 나서 다시 술을 마시고…… 아내 말마따나 난 영영 폐인이 된 셈인

understand they had a life of extreme poverty and loneliness after she became a widow at a young age. That son who, Haenam-Daek would always say with pride, was determined enough to finish high school despite their financial situation, got a job right away at some foundry in the Gwangcheon-dong industrial district and became a special techni-cian in no time, left the house as usual with his lunch pail one late spring morning of nineteen-eighty, and is yet to return for some reason. Without any witness who has seen him or any letter saying I'm alive and well, that son of hers, with a nice high forehead, has been missing for four years. Because of that, shedding tears is a daily activity for Haenam-Daek. She has COPD on top of it, so listen-ing to her almost lose her breath letting out coughs that sound as if her throat were being scraped with a rake really drives you insane. Myeong-gi-yaah. Aao ya uncarin', cole-hearted bastaard. What kind of crap are ya up to, ripping yer mum's heart apaaart? Where are ya when I'm dying heere? Oh my sonny booyy. Day and night, Haenam-Daek would mutter those tedious words to herself in her room like reciting an incantation. I truly dreaded her mutterings. During the day, it was just the two

지도 모르죠.

 그러니까 그날은 아마 지난주 일요일이었을 겁니다. 아
내가 낮에도 집에 있었으니까. 언제나처럼 아침을 거른
채 누워 있던 나는 잠결에 어디선가 들려오는 괴이한 신
음 소리에 소스라쳐 놀라 눈을 떴지요. 명기야이. 아이고
오. 이 불쌍한 자석아이. 울음도 같고 노랫가락도 같은 청
승맞은 목소리는 옆방에서 들려오고 있었습니다. 난 몸을
벌떡 일으켰다가 다시 드러눕고 말았지요. 식은땀이 온몸
으로 질펀해 있더군요. 곁에서 바느질을 하고 있던 아내
가 오히려 놀랐는지, 무슨 흉한 꿈이라도 꿨느냐며 묻더
군요.

 그 청승맞은 넋두리는 해남댁이라고, 오래전부터 우리
집 문간방에 세 들어 살고 있는 늙은 여자의 음성이었습
니다. 환갑을 갓 넘긴 나이에 벌써 얼굴 여기저기 저승꽃
이 피기 시작해서 얼핏 보아서는 칠순이 훨씬 지난 노파
로 여겨질 정도죠. 해남댁에겐 명기라고 하는 스물두어
살 난 아들이 하나 있었는데, 젊어서 남편과 사별한 뒤 두
모자는 밑구멍이 째지도록 가난하고 외롭게 살아왔다더
군요. 고등학교를 어렵사리 마치자마자 광천동 공단의 무
슨 주물 공장인가에 나다니기 시작해서 어느덧 기술자가

of us in the house, so I had to endure those pitiful cries that would recur almost on a daily basis. On such days, I'd always dream I would throw her down and kill her by strangling her like crazy with my two hands. Even harder to take were her bizarre fits, which would hit every once in a while. In the middle of the night, out of nowhere, she'd swing open the door loudly and drift out to the yard, screaming Myeong-gi-yaah, ya came baaack, my baby has fine'ly come back to his mum, he haaazz. Then without fail, she would open the gate wide. Many a time my wife and I would wake up with a jolt and get all worked up thinking something terrible must have happened. Then we'd look out and see that poor old woman standing blankly in the darkness by the gate, with her hair all disheveled like a bird's nest. She'd say she thought her son had come back. She definitely heard him call out with a bright, vivid voice, she'd say. Nooh, Fer shure. I had a dream, and that bastard was standing there holding a big bunch of white snowball flowers with his two arms and said, Mum, it's meey, Myeong-gi. I'm baack, and started walkin' toward me in big steps. Then I opened my eyes quick-like, and fer real the gate was shaking to-and-fro and the kid was calling

71

되었다고 늘 해남댁이 자랑하던 아들은 팔십 년 그 늦은 봄 어느 날 아침에 언제나처럼 도시락을 싸서 들고 집을 나선 뒤로는 무슨 영문인지 영영 돌아오지 않고 있었습니다. 어디서 그를 보았다는 사람도, 나 여기 살아 있노라는 편지 한 장도 없는 채로 그 이마가 훤칠한 아들은 벌써 사 년째 행방이 묘연했지요. 그 때문에 해남댁은 날이면 날마다 눈물을 쥐어짜는 게 일이었어요. 해소병까지 있어서 목구멍을 갈퀴로 긁어내리는 듯한 기침을 숨넘어가게 토해내는 소리를 듣고 있노라면 정말이지 환장할 지경이지 뭡니까. 명기야이, 시상에나 무심허고 야속시런 놈의 자석아이. 니기 에미 애간장이 녹아서 다 죽어가는 줄 모르고 어디서 뭘 하고 자빠졌단 말이냐이. 아이고오, 내 새끼야이. 해남댁은 밤이고 낮이고 가리지 않고 무슨 주문을 외는 듯한 그 지겨운 넋두리를 혼자 방 안에서 씨부렁대곤 했지요. 난 그 넋두리를 끔찍하게 싫어했습니다. 낮엔 해남댁과 나, 그렇게 단 둘이서만 남아 있어야 했으므로 거의 하루도 빠짐없이 되풀이되는 그 처량한 울음을 참아내야 했다니까요. 그런 날이면 꿈속에서 어김없이 그 늙은이를 쓰려뜨려 놓고 나는 두 손으로 미친 듯 목을 졸라 죽이는 꿈을 꾸었습니다. 더더욱 견디기 어려운 것은 가

me, his mum... Like this, Haenam-Daek would insist on the story that made no sense from the very beginning. But the two of us knew only too well how futile it was for the poor old woman to keep on waiting. For it was almost impossible that her son, who hadn't been heard from at all in four years since that spring day of that year, would ever come back. Auntie, please calm down. Your son will come back soon. How could such a dedicated young man and good son ever forget about his mother? I can't say for certain but I bet he's working hard somewhere to become a success so that he can come back and take you back with him. That was the only lie my wife and I could manage to tell Haenam-Daek. But whenever I did, my throat would get prickly all of a sudden, I'd have trouble breathing, and my chest would feel suffocated. Yes, it was the poison gas. That damned thing would always hide without a trace, then bolt out like a devious murderer and squeeze down on my neck.

That was the case on that day. Hearing the old woman's moaning chant that went aoh ma, aoh ma, I lay there for a good while, my entire body dripping with cold sweat. My wife seemed to be sitting by the bed and mending the broken seams in my

끔씩 도지곤 하는 해남댁의 괴이한 발작이었지요. 느닷없이 한밤중에 문을 꽈당 열어젖히고는 징정징정 마당으로 뛰쳐나오며, 명기야이, 니가 왔구나아, 내 새끼가 인자서 에미를 찾아왔구나아, 하고 고함을 치는 겁니다. 그리고는 영락없이 대문을 활짝 열어젖히는 거예요. 그때마다 나와 아내는 잠결에 후다닥 일어나, 무슨 난리가 난 게 아닌가 해서 가슴을 벌렁거린 적이 한두 번이 아니었습니다. 내다보면 그 불쌍한 늙은이는 깜깜한 어둠 속에서 까치집같이 산발한 머리꼴을 하고 대문 앞에서 우두커니 서 있곤 했습니다. 아들이 찾아온 줄만 알았다지 뭡니까. 분명히 또렷하고 생생한 음성으로 부르는 소리를 들었다는 거지요. 아니여. 틀림없어. 꿈을 꾸었는디, 그놈이 하얀 밥티꽃을 가슴에 한아름 보듬고 서서는, 어무니 나여라우, 명기가 돌아왔어라우, 하면서 내 앞으로 뚬벅뚬벅 걸어오는 것이여. 그러다가 퍼뜩 눈을 떠 보니께 진짜로 대문이 와랑와랑 흔들림서 그 자석이 에미를 부른 것이여…… 이런 식으로 해남댁은 애당초 말도 안 되는 얘기를 막무가내로 우겨대곤 했습니다. 하지만 우리 둘은 그 불쌍한 늙은 여자의 기다림이 얼마나 부질없는 짓인가를 잘 알고 있었지요. 그해 봄날 이후로 사 년째가 되도록 영영 소식

shirts. On Sundays, she would always diligently do the heaps of laundry and clean every corner of the house. Lying there and watching her bulging belly, due within the next couple of months, and her pale fingers moving about above it, holding the needle, I suddenly had a delusion that the sharp tip of the needle, which my wife was pushing in stitch by stitch, was aimed at her big belly, poking deeply into it. I sat up instantly with a shudder. Aoh ma, aoh ma, that dammed bastard sonneee... as soon as I heard those dreaded moans and chants, my nostrils started to sting. It was poison gas. Poison gas. And seeing me so flustered, of course my wife treated me like I'd lost my head. Geesh. That's my wife: Ms. Obtuse. She said she did not smell a whiff of that foul and awful odor. I mean, what do you say to that? But on this day I had particular trouble with the smell of the poison gas. I was almost throwing up.

I ran out right away, roamed the streets aimlessly, then got on any bus. It was pretty crowded although it was the weekend. I take it there was a postseason baseball game at the Mudeung Stadium. I mindlessly looked up and saw that all those people had their wrists stuck in rows of white handles

이 없는 아들이 다시 돌아오리라고는 거의 믿기 어려웠으니까요. 아주머니, 이젠 그만 진정하세요. 아드님은 곧 돌아올 겁니다. 그렇게 성실하고 효성스런 젊은이가 설마 어머니를 잊을 리가 있을라구요. 모르면 몰라도 성공해서 돌아와 어머니를 모시려고 어디선가 열심히 일하고 있을 겁니다. 아내와 내가 해남댁에게 해줄 수 있는 거짓말이라곤 고작 그뿐이었습니다. 한데, 그때마다 난 목구멍이 갑자기 따끔따끔해져 오면서 숨쉬기가 거북해지고 가슴이 답답해지곤 했어요. 그래요. 바로 그 독가스였습니다. 그놈은 언제나 흔적조차 없이 어딘가에 숨어 있다가도 음흉한 살인자처럼 느닷없이 뛰쳐나와 목을 컥컥 짓눌러대곤 했으니까요.

이날도 마찬가지였어요. 아이고오, 아이고오, 하는 그 늙은 여자의 흥타령을 들으면서 나는 한참이나 온몸에 식은땀을 흥건히 적시며 누워 있었지요. 아내는 머리맡에 앉아서 실밥이 터져 나간 내 셔츠 겨드랑이를 꿰매고 있는 눈치였지요. 일요일이면 언제나 밀린 빨래를 하고 집안 구석구석 청소를 하는 것이 부지런한 그녀의 일이었습니다. 해산일이 두 달도 미처 안 남은 아내의 부풀어 오른 배, 그리고 그 위에서 움직이고 있는 바늘을 쥔 하얀 손가

that looked like links. That's right. All of us were prisoners who had been arrested. Confined inside the bus, we were all being transferred with white handcuffs around our wrists to who-knows-where, tacitly, without a word of protest or struggle. Looking at the numerous hands hanging in the air like corpses exposing their pale rotten flesh, I had that feeling again where the poison gas was choking my throat. I rushed off the bus when it arrived at the governor's office.

The streets of a weekend afternoon were undulating with passers-by on a leisurely stroll. The sky was a bit overcast but rain wasn't in the picture. Via the crosswalk in front of the Jeonil Building, I headed in the direction of the NFFC. Standing on the previously mentioned steps, I stared at the square and the fountain in front of me for quite a while. On this day, particularly, water was gushing out powerfully from the fountain in the center of the square so that you could hear the streams fall. It was a soft yet obstinately tenacious sound, like the breathing of someone just about to die. Facing the view in the square that some would describe as extremely peaceful, I could not get out of my head the horrifying scene I'd witnessed right there on that

락들을 바라보며 누워 있다가 나는 불현듯 아내가 한 땀 한 땀 밀어 넣고 있는 그 날카로운 바늘 끝이 영락없이 아내의 부른 배를 노리며 푹푹푹 들어가 박히고 있는 듯한 착각에 몸서리를 치며 벌떡 일어나 버렸습니다. 아이고오, 아이고. 이 몹쓸 자석아이…… 벽 저쪽에선 다시 지겨운 넋두리와 흥타령이 들려왔고 문득 콧구멍이 매캐해지기 시작했지요. 독가스였습니다. 독가스. 허둥대는 날 붙잡고 아내는 버릇처럼 정신 나간 사람 취급을 하려 들겠지요. 원, 세상에. 내 아내는 그렇게 둔한 여자랍니다. 그 지독하고 끔찍스런 냄새를 전혀 모르겠다지 뭡니까. 내 참, 기가 막혀서. 하지만 난 이날은 유난히도 독가스 냄새를 견딜 수가 없었어요. 구역질이 날 지경이었지요.

밖으로 이내 뛰쳐나가 무작정 거리를 쏘다니다가 아무 버스에나 올라탔지요. 휴일인데도 차 안은 붐볐습니다. 프로야구 결승전이 무등경기장에서 있다나요. 무심코 고개를 들어 보니, 거기 무수한 사람들의 손목이 하얀 고리형의 손잡이에 하나같이 나란히 꿰어져 있더군요. 그래요. 모두가 체포된 수인들이었어요. 차 안에 갇힌 우리 모두는 팔목에 하얀 수갑이 채워진 채 어딘지도 모를 곳으로 한마디의 항변도 몸부림도 없이 묵묵히 압송되어져 가

rainy night. Was it really an illusion? Had I seen something that wasn't there in the middle of the pouring rainstorm? I stood in the middle of the crowded street, yet I felt as though I were still having an unsettling and fearsome dream.

Meanwhile, arrays of cars kept passing by swiftly, and like ants, passers-by crawled out from big and small streets of the city in an endless flow. At bus stops, whenever a bus showed up with a number sign on it just like the ones in concentration camps, people kept running in droves toward what was to transport them. I felt like asking those citizens who were pushing and shoving and bumping into one another, scurrying to get on the buses as if someone were blowing a whistle like crazy behind them or chasing them: Do you know by any chance the whereabouts of the numerous people who disappeared in long lines through that square there in May of that year? Where have they gone, with those soft and vivid red petals in their mouths? And why are none of these countless people back? Why do we still have nothing on the only child of the old Haenam-Daek...? But I ended up not being able to say anything before coming back home.

I spent the next two full days lying, getting by

고 있었다구요. 썩어 문드러진 뱃가죽을 허옇게 드러낸 채 시체처럼 허공에 매달려 있는 그 숱한 손들을 바라보고 있으려니 또 독가스가 목을 짓눌러대는 느낌이었습니다. 차가 도청 앞에 이르렀을 때 허둥지둥 뛰어내리고 말았습니다.

휴일 하오의 거리는 한가로운 걸음의 행인들로 출렁이고 있었습니다. 하늘은 흐린 편이었지만 비가 올 듯한 날씨는 아니었지요. 전일 빌딩 앞 횡단보도를 건너 수협 건물 쪽으로 갔습니다. 난 예의 그 계단에 서서 꽤 오랫동안 눈앞의 광장과 분수대를 우두커니 바라보았지요. 이날따라 광장 중앙의 분수대는 시원스레 물을 뿜어 올리고 있더군요. 질주하는 차량들의 소음에 섞여 쏴쏴쏴쏴 하는 물줄기의 낙하음이 들렸습니다. 그것은 마치 지금 마악 임종하는 사람의 숨결처럼 나지막하면서도 집요하도록 끈질긴 소리였지요. 어찌 보면 지극히 평화스럽기만 한 광장의 풍경을 대하고 있으려니까 자꾸만 그 비 오는 날 밤, 바로 그 자리에서 보았던 소름 끼치는 광경이 뇌리에서 지워지지가 않았습니다. 그것은 정말 환영이었을까. 억수같이 쏟아지는 비바람 속에서 얼결에 헛것을 보았던 것일까. 나는 북적이는 한길에 서서 여전히 어수선하고

only on water. Even when I was lying motionless, with my mouth open as wide as it would go, my breathing was constricted, and there was an odd sound from my throat, like air leaking. That foul smell—I have no idea where or how it all started—jumped on my chest while I collapsed, choking my neck endlessly. My eyes became bloodshot, and my throat swelled up so much that I had difficulty swallowing. Oh, so this is how I die finally. This is how I go. When I thought that, I could not help feeling tremendously vexed and unjustified. That's right. There was no way I was going to die just like that. I thought to myself I could never close my eyes in vain like this. I got up with vigor and got out my sketch pad. I was drawing my first cartoon in a truly long time. I breezily sketched in the scary scene from that rainy night, the rows of people who were being led somewhere with red petals stuck all over their bodies. Then, I found a board and nails to make a sign, where I wrote the following in thick letters:

"I am dying every day from an unidentified poison gas and toxic chemicals. Please save me.—Third day of fasting"

I put a string through the cartoon to hang it from

흉흉한 꿈을 꾸고 있는 듯한 느낌이었습니다.

그사이에도 차량의 행렬이 분주히 스쳐 지나가고 시가지의 이 골목 저 골목으로부터 행인들이 개미 떼처럼 구물구물 기어 나와 끊임없이 흐르고 있었습니다. 정류장에 선 수용소 막사의 번호판만 같은 숫자표를 달고 자신들을 실어 갈 시내버스가 나타날 때마다 사람들은 그리로 우루루 몰려가곤 했습니다. 마치 등 뒤에서 누군가가 미친 듯 호루라기를 불어대기라도 하듯 저마다 어깨를 밀고 부딪치며 쫓기듯이 허겁지겁 차에 오르고 있는 시민들을 붙잡고 나는 이렇게 묻고 싶었습니다. 그해 오월, 바로 저 광장을 돌아 길다랗게 열을 지어 사라져버린 숱한 사람들의 행방을 행여 알고 있느냐고. 선연하도록 붉고 고운 꽃이 파리를 입에 물고 그들은 대관절 어디로 가버린 것이냐고. 그리고 그 많은 사람들은 왜 아무도 돌아오지 않느냐고. 어째서 해남댁 늙은이의 외아들은 아직까지 소식조차 알 수 없는 거냐고…… 하지만 끝내 아무 말도 해보지 못하고 집으로 되돌아오고 말았습니다.

그날부터 나는 꼬박 이틀을 물만 마시며 누워 있었습니다. 입을 잔뜩 벌리고 꼼짝없이 누워 있어도 호흡이 막혀오고 목구멍에서 바람이 새는 듯한 이상한 소리가 났습니

my neck, and went out into the streets holding the sign in my hand. Then I got up on the steps in front of the Chungjang-ro post office, the most crowded spot, and stood there motionless for hours. People gathered, pointed at me and giggled. Some dropped coins, some tossed me gum, some threw out their used straws at me, and some even held my hand without saying a word, nodded, or shook my hand before continuing on their way. Through it all, I always stood motionless, like a mannequin. I did the same thing the next day and went in front of the post office.

"...Please save me.—Fourth day of fasting"

I went out to the same spot the following day. Until the fifth day, I had not eaten anything. But on the afternoon of that final day, while I was standing there alone, holding up the sign, those people came to get me...

Well, that's all. This is all you'll get out of me, Doctor. Now I don't want to say anything any more. Understand? I will not go any further. Heheheh. But you know, Doctor, there is one thing I'd really like to know. Well, let's see. Do you think I'll be able to draw cartoons again? I mean, will I be able to draw

다. 어디서 어떻게 시작되었는지조차 알 수 없는 그 지독한 냄새는 쓰러져 누운 내 가슴 위에 올라타서 끊임없이 목을 조르고 또 졸랐지요. 눈알이 벌겋게 충혈되면서 이윽고는 목구멍 안까지 퉁퉁 부어올라 침을 삼키기마저 어려워지더군요. 아아, 기어이 난 이렇게 죽어가는구나. 이렇게 죽고 마는구나. 그런 생각이 들자 나는 무지무지하게 분하고 억울하다는 느낌을 참을 수가 없더군요. 그래요. 난 그대로 죽을 수는 없었습니다. 절대로 이렇게 허망하게 눈을 감아서는 안 된다는 생각이 들더군요. 나는 자리를 박차고 일어나 스케치북을 꺼냈지요. 실로 오랜만에 그려보는 만화였습니다. 나는 거기에 그 비 오는 날 밤의 무서운 광경을, 꽃잎을 온몸에 붉게 붙인 채 어디론가 끌려가고 있는 사람들의 행렬을 쓱쓱 그려 넣었습니다. 그러고 나서 판자와 못을 찾아내어 표지판을 하나 만들고 거기에 굵은 글씨로 이렇게 썼습니다.

"저는 지금 정체를 알 수 없는 독가스와 독극물로 인해 날마다 죽어가고 있습니다. 제발 저를 살려주십시오. ─단식 사흘째"

만화엔 실을 꿰어서 목에 걸고, 손에는 표지판을 든 채 나는 거리로 나갔습니다. 그리고 행인들로 가장 붐비는

those damned straight lines without using a ruler just like that, the way I used to do? And above all, from where do you think this poison gas, this utterly abhorrent and awful smell of poison gas wafts in like pollen, huh? Why I have to be the only one to go through such suffering when everyone else is living on like nothing is wrong, I truly have no idea, Doctor.

1) The local specialty of Yeonggwang, a seaside city in Jeollanam-do Province, dried yellow croakers are sold in packs of twenty as two rows of ten fish tied together by straw strings.
2) Koreans associate the wearing of surgical masks in public with cold weather, when some people don them so as not to catch or give a cold.

Translated by Chris Choi

충장로 우체국 앞 계단에 올라서서 몇 시간을 꼼짝없이 서 있었지요. 사람들이 모여들어 저마다 손가락질을 해대며 낄낄거렸습니다. 동전을 떨어뜨려 놓고 가는 사람, 껌을 던져주는 사람, 음료수를 마시고 나서 빨대를 내던져주는 사람, 더러는 말없이 내 손을 찾아 잡고 고개를 끄덕이며 악수를 해주고 지나가는 사람들도 있었지요. 그래도 나는 언제나 마네킹처럼 꼼짝하지 않고 서 있었습니다. 그 이튿날도 마찬가지로 우체국 앞에 나갔지요.

"……저를 살려주세요.─단식 나흘째"

그다음 날도 역시 그리로 나갔습니다. 닷새째가 되는 그날까지도 난 전혀 아무것도 입에 대지 않은 채로였지요. 그런데 바로 그 마지막 날 오후에 혼자 표지판을 치켜들고 서 있으려니까 바로 그자들이 나를 데리러 왔던 것이었습니다……

자아, 이것뿐입니다. 선생님이 내가 알아낼 수 있는 사실은 모두 이것밖에 없어요. 이젠 아무 얘기도 하고 싶지 않습니다. 아시겠어요? 더는 계속하지 않을 거라구요. 으흐흐홋. 하지만 말예요, 선생님. 꼭 한 가지만 알고 싶은 게 있기는 합니다. 저, 말이죠. 나는 다시 만화를 그릴 수가 있을까요? 자를 대지 않고서도 그 빌어먹을 놈의 직선을 예전처럼 쓱쓱 그려낼 수 있겠느냐구요. 그리고 무엇보다도 이 독가스, 지긋지긋하고 끔찍스러운 이 독가스 냄새는 대관절 어디서 어떻게 꽃가루같이 풀풀풀 날아오는 것일까요, 네. 다른 사람들은 모두 아무렇지도 않게 살아가고 있는데 어째서 하필 나 혼자만 이렇게 고통을 당해야 하는 것인지, 정말이지 난 모르겠다니까요. 선생님.

『직선과 독가스』, 문학사상사, 1989

해설

Afterword

1980년 5월 광주의 비망록

양진오(문학평론가)

1980년 5월 광주가 무엇을 의미하는지 아는 한국인들은 광주를 단지 남도의 한 도시로 이해하지 않는다. 아니, 이건 이해의 문제가 아니다. 적지 않은 한국인들은 지금도 광주라는 말을 듣는 순간, 그 말에서 가혹한 폭력의 잔상을 느낀다. 이 가혹한 폭력의 실체를 여기서 일일이 설명하는 건 가능하지 않다. 자신들만의 절대 권력을 구축할 목적으로 광기의 폭력을 주도한 신군부 세력 그리고 이들에 편승한 다양한 내부 협조자들. 그들이 만들어 낸건 진실의 봉쇄이자 끊임없는 왜곡이다. 그들은 광주에서 1980년 5월의 시간을 아예 지워버리려 했다. 마치, 아무일도 없었던 것처럼 말이다.

Reminder of Gwangju, May 1980

Yang Jin-o (literary critic)

Those Koreans who know the significance of
Gwangju of May 1980, understand the place to be
more than merely a city in a southern Province.
Well, it is more than a matter of understanding.
More than a few Koreans, upon hearing the word
Gwangju, sense the afterimage of brutal violence
from the word. It is not possible to explain in detail
the identity of that brutal violence here. What those
of the new military regime who led the deranged
violence in order to establish their own absolute
power, and the various internal collaborators who
jumped on their bandwagon, made was an obstruction and endless distortion of the truth. They tried

모든 작가가 그렇지는 않지만 진실이 봉쇄되는 지점에서 마치 운명처럼 자신의 문학을 상상하고 기획하는 작가들이 있다. 이 상상과 기획은 물론 그 자체로 고역이다. 작가는 작가이기 이전에 먼저 자신이 속한 세상과 큰 마찰 없이 지내고 싶은 자연인이 아니던가. 그렇기에 작가가 진실이 봉쇄된 자리에서 자신의 문학을 열어간다는 건 분명 쉬운 일이 아니다. 더구나 진실을 봉쇄하는 주체가 가공할 권력의 소유자들이라면 작가의 부담은 더 말할 필요가 없다. 여기서 우리는 임철우를 다시 주목해야 한다. 임철우는 광주의 진실이 봉쇄된 저 1980년대부터 이미 광주를 자신의 문학적 자산으로 받아들인 작가였다. 그런데 이 받아들임은 소재주의적 접근과는 질적으로 구분되는 장관을 훗날 연출하게 되니, 임철우는 본질적으로 1980년 5월 광주를 자신의 운명으로 받아들여 문학적 성취를 이뤄낸 작가라 하겠다.

「직선과 독가스」는 5월 광주를 직접적으로 이야기할 수 없는 폭압의 시대를 배경으로 발표된 광주의 비망록이다. 그 폭압의 시대에서 광주의 진실은 절대 발설되지 말아야 하는 금기 중의 금기였다. 그러나 절대 발설되지 않는 금기는 존재하지 않는 법. 문학은 다양한 방식에 기대어 이

to erase for good from Gwangju the time of May 1980 as if nothing had ever happened there then.

Although not the case for every writer, there are those who seem to take as their fate to imagine and formulate their literary output from the point of obstruction of the truth. The imagining and the formulating are of course a hassle in themselves. For a writer is first a natural person who should want to live without big problems with the world to which he or she belongs, before being a writer. Thus, for a writer to start her or his literary journey at the place of obstruction of the truth cannot be an easy task. The pressure on the writer becomes all the greater when the agency that obstructs the truth rests with those who possess fearsome powers. This is where we need to turn our attention to Lim Chul-woo again. Lim Chul-woo was a writer who had already accepted Gwangju as his literary resource from the 1980s when its truth was obstructed. And this acceptance would later produce splendid results qualitatively distinct from a subject-centered approach, bestowing upon Im the title of the writer who had literary accomplishment by accepting as his fate the Gwangju of May 1980.

"Straight Lines and Poison Gas" is a reminder of

금기를 뒤집고 증언해 왔으니 임철우의 「직선과 독가스」
도 그 예에 해당한다. 「직선과 독가스」는 5월 광주를 낳은
한국 사회를 감금과 실종의 닫힌 사회로 비유한다. 그런
데 임철우는 이 감금과 실종의 문제를 현대 사회에 속한
인간이라면 누구나 마주하게 된다는 식의 추상적 상황의
문제로 환원하지는 않는다. 임철우는 이 감금과 실종의
문제를 1980년 5월 광주로 표상되는 구체적 현실과 연관
시키고 있으니 이 소설에 등장하는 독가스, 분단, 구금, 광
장과 같은 언어적 표현들은 예외 없이 「직선과 독가스」의
당대적 성격을 고조시킨다. 이 언어적 표현을 따라 「직선
과 독가스」를 읽다보면 우리는 "한 두름의 굴비처럼 길다
랗게 꿰어진" 채 "한 줄로 길게 늘어서서 느릿느릿 걸음
을 옮길 때마다 쩔걱대는 차꼬 소리와 땅에 끌리는 쇠사
슬 소리"의 주인공들, 그러니까 그 참혹한 5월에 사라진
익명의 주인공들을 만나게 된다.

이 소설의 스토리는 복잡하지 않다. 지방 H신문사에 소
속되어 만평을 그리는 허화백이 어느 날 정체불명의 사내
들에게 붙잡혀 낯선 하얀 방으로 끌려간다. 추악한 권력
의 고문실을 환기시키는 이 하얀 방에 감금된 허화백은
정체불명의 사내들에게서 "마을 사람들 목숨 여럿을 끊어

Gwangju set against the epochal background of vio-
lent oppression where the Gwangju of May could
not be mentioned explicitly. In that period of
oppression, the truth about Gwangju was the taboo
of taboos that was not to be divulged. But there is
no such thing as a secret that is never divulged.
Literature has overthrown and testified on this taboo
relying on various methods, one example of which
is "Straight Lines and Poison Gas" by Lim Chul-woo.
"Straight Lines and Poison Gas" compares the
Korean society that gave birth to the Gwangju of
May with a closed one with confinement and loss.
But Lim Chul-woo does not reduce this issue of
confinement and loss to one of an abstract circum-
stance that any person living in the modern world
faces at some point. Lim Chul-woo associates this
issue of confinement and loss with the specific reality represented by the Gwangju of May 1980 through
such linguistic expressions as poison gas, division,
detention and square in "Straight Lines and Poison
Gas," intensifying the characteristics of the day without fail. Following these linguistic expressions while
reading "Straight Lines and Poison Gas," we
encounter the anonymous figures who disappeared
in that atrocious May, those who were "roped

놓은 채 지리산 어딘가로 야밤에 흔적도 없이 도망쳐 버린" 큰아버지 허창수의 존재를 환기 받는다. 과거 한국전쟁에 관여한 좌익계 인사로 추정되는 큰아버지가 반공주의 국가의 국민인 허화백으로서는 부담스러운 존재였으니, 허화백은 하얀 방에서 자신이 권력의 감시에 완전히 포박되어 있다는 것을 확연히 깨닫는다.

　어렵사리 하얀 방에서 풀려난 허화백은 결코 자유를 구가할 수 없는 "체포된 수인"처럼 재현되고 있지만 사실 허화백이 더 주목되는 이유는 그해 5월에 행방이 묘연한 실종자들의 존재를 지속적으로 추적하는 탐문자의 성격을 띠기 때문이다. 물론 이 탐문은 알레고리의 수준을 상회하지는 않는다. 소속 신문사에서 해고된 허화백은 그해 5월 실종된 광주 시민들을 환영의 형식으로 목격하거나 아니면 절대 권력의 후각적 상징인 독가스 냄새에 괴롭게 반응하는 방식으로 실종자들의 존재를 환기시킨다. 그리고 그 실종자들에 대한 환기는 "피의 꽃잎을 온몸에 붉게 붙인 채 어디론가 끌려가는 사람들의 행렬"을 허화백이 만화로 그린 후 이를 들고 충장로 우체국 앞 계단에 올라서는 장면과 뒤이어 낯선 이들에게 피체되는 장면에서 더욱 절정을 보인다. 1980년 5월 광주가 남긴 상처에서 자

together like a package of dried yellow croakers" and from whom came "the clanks of fetters and the metal chains dragging on the ground" "with every slow steps they took, stretched in a line."

The plot of this story is uncomplicated. Comic artist Heo, who draws political cartoons for a local newspaper H, is arrested by unidentified men and dragged to a strange white room one day. Confined in this white room, which is reminiscent of torture rooms of despicable power, Heo is reminded by the unidentified men of the existence of Heo Seong-su, his "uncle who had caused the deaths of many villagers and" who had "fled overnight to some place in Jiri Mountain." The uncle, assumed to have belonged to the political left who got involved in the Korean War, was a burdensome figure to the narrator Heo, who thus realizes that he is completely caught by the surveillance of power in the white room.

After his difficult release, Heo is depicted as an "arrested prisoner" who can never sing praises of liberty, but in fact the reason he gets more attention is that he takes on the characteristics of a searcher who continuously chases the whereabouts of those who have been missing since May of "that" year.

신의 문학을 열어간 임철우. 「직선과 독가스」는 임철우의
문학이 광주의 상처에 아주 깊게 이어져 있다는 것을 입
증하는 탁월한 사례이다.

This search, of course, does not exceed the level of allegory. After getting fired by the paper, he either witnesses those Gwangju residents who disappeared that May in the form of hallucination, or gives as a reminder of the missing persons by reacting in agony to the smell of poison gas, the olfactory symbol of the absolute power. And that reminder of the missing persons reaches its climax in the scene where Heo climbs the steps in front of the Chunjang-ro post office holding the cartoon he has drawn of "the rows of people who were being led somewhere with red petals stuck all over their bodies" and the subsequent scene where he is captured by strange men. Lim Chul-woo took as his literary starting point the wound left by the Gwangju of May 1980. "Straight Lines and Poison Gas" is an excellent example proving that his works have a deep connection to the wound of Gwangju.

비평의 목소리

Critical Acclaim

임철우의 소설에 있어서 광주는 원점에 해당된다. 그의 소설은 광주에서부터 흘러나왔고 광주를 향해 가고 있다. 임철우의 소설이 보여주는 탁월한 서정성조차도 광주 체험의 산물이다. 광주에 대한 그의 의식이 폭력에 대한 분노보다 자기 반성적인 부끄러움에 가깝다는 점은 주목을 요한다. 그의 서정성은 부끄러움의 또 다른 표현인 셈이다.

광주가 금지된 상징이었을 때, 임철우는 그 상징의 성에서 탈출해 나온 사람처럼 알레고리와 비유를 통한 시적이고 우회적인 방식으로 광주의 문제를 제기했었다.

서영채

Gwangju serves as the point of origin for Lim Chul-woo's fictions. His works started from Gwangju, which is also where they are headed. Even the outstanding lyricism on display in Lim Chul-woo's fictions is a product of the Gwangju experience. It should be noted that his awareness of Gwangju is closer to self-repentant shame than wrath at violence. His lyricism is another channel of expression for shame.

At the time when Gwangju was a forbidden symbol, Lim Chul-woo raised the issue of Gwangju like a person who had escaped that symbolic fortress by the poetic and circuitous means of allegory and

작가 임철우는 역사의 비극적 사건과 같은 다소 무거운 제재를 통하여 척박한 삶의 현실과 냉혹한 이념의 허상이 얽어내는, 인간과 정치의 금속성 가득한 역사적 교직물을 직조해왔다. 특히 그는 역사의 비극성에 처한 인간들의 절규, 자의식, 혼돈, 절망과 다층적인 현실의 비정함과 기만을 파헤치면서 역사적 현실에 대한 통렬한 비판의식과 심오한 문제의식을 드러내왔는데, 이러한 중후한 주제와 작품세계를 지닌 그의 80년대 단편소설들이야말로 임철우 창작의 출발점이자 작품의 본령으로 인정받고 있다.

김경원

그러나 이제 우리는 조금은 다른 각도에서의 검토가 필요하다고 생각한다. 그런 생각은 임철우가 90년대 들어 발표한 두 권의 장편소설 『그 섬에 가고 싶다』와 『등대 아래서 휘파람』으로부터 비롯된다. 이 두 권의 장편소설은 작가의 유소년기를 다룬 자전적 성장소설로서 광주 체험의 암시가 거의 나타나지 않을뿐더러 종래의 임철우 소설과는 사뭇 판이하게, 전적인 화해 지향의 세계를 이루고 있다. 이 장편소설들은 여러 가지 의문을 불러일으킨다. 이는 임철우 소설의 획기적인 변모를 뜻하는 것일까. 그

analogy.

Seo Yeong-chae

Through somewhat heavy subject matters such as tragic events in history, the writer Lim Chul-woo has been weaving a historical metallic mix of humankind and politics made from the intertwining of the barren reality of life and the ruthless illusion of ideology. He has especially been exhibiting a profound consciousness and a sharply critical mind with respect to historical reality by exposing the cries, the self-consciousness, the confusion, and the despair of those faced with the tragic nature of history as well as the heartlessness and deception of the multilayered reality. His short stories from the 1980s, with their literary domain consisting of such grave themes, are acknowledged as the very starting point for Lim Chul-woo's literary creativity and the proper function of his works.

Kim Gyeong-won

But I believe we need a review from a bit different angle now. That belief stems from two novels he published in the 1990s, *I Want to Go to That Island* and *Whistling under the Lighthouse.* Dealing with

렇다면 그것은 어떠한 변모인가. 자세히 들여다보면, 그러나 많은 모티프들을 등단작 이래의 종래의 세계와 공유하고 있는 것도 사실이다.

성민엽

the author's childhood and boyhood, these two autobiographical coming-of-age novels barely hint at the Gwangju experience, while at the same time presenting a world wholly committed to reconciliation, quite a departure from his previous works. These novels raise a number of questions. Do these mean a momentous transformation in Lim Chul-woo's fictions? If so, what kind of transformation would that be? A closer look, however, shows us that these novels have many motifs in common with his previous domain beginning with his inaugural work.

Seong Min-yeop

임철우

1954년 10월 15일 임철우는 전남 완도군 금일면 평일도 일정리에서 태어난다. 바다가 내려다보이는 백여 채의 초가집 중 하나에서 그는 색깔과 냄새로 가득 찬 유년을 보낸다. 평일도는 임철우가 지속적으로 변주한 문학적 자산이다. 『그 섬에 가고 싶다』 『등대 아래서 휘파람』 『붉은 산 흰 새』 등은 평일도가 없었다면 탄생하기 어려운 작품들이다. 1963년 전남도청으로 발령받은 부친을 따라 임철우는 광주로 이사한다. 광주에서 초등학교, 중학교, 고등학교를 졸업한 임철우는 1973년 전남대학교 영문학과에 입학한다. 휴학과 군복무를 마친 임철우가 대학에 복학한 해는 1978년이다. 복학한 임철우는 광주의 마당극 놀이패인 광대에 합류하지만 더는 마당극에 몰두할 수 없었다. 5월 광주가 터진 까닭이다. 임철우는 5월 광주를 체험하며 인간에 대한 한없는 절망을 느끼면서도 인간에 대한 끝없는 애정과 믿음을 터득한다. 임철우의 문학은 바로 이 애정과 믿음에서 시작하고 있다.

1981년 임철우는 《서울신문》 신춘문예에 「개도둑」으로

Lim Chul-woo

Lim Chul-woo was born in Iljeong-ri, Pyeong-il Island, Geumil-myeon, Wando-gun in South Jeolla Province on the 15th of October, 1954. He spent his childhood filled with colors and scents in one of the hundred or so houses with thatched roofs overlooking the sea. Pyeong-il Island is a literary resource from which Lim Chul-woo has continuously generated variations. Without Pyeong-il Island, such works as *I Want to Go to That Island, Whistling under the Lighthouse*, and *Red Mountain, White Bird* could not have been written. In 1963, Lim Chul-woo moved to Gwangju when his father was transferred to the Provincial House. After finishing elementary, middle and high schools in Gwangju, Lim Chul-woo entered the English Department of Chonnam National University in 1973. After a leave of absence and military duty, Lim Chul-woo returned to college in 1978. As a returnee, Lim Chul-woo joined Gwangdae, a Gwangju madang-geuk (the people's theater) crew, but would not be able to focus on it for long. This was because it was

등단한다. 등단한 해부터 임철우는 「그들의 새벽」 「뒤안에는 바람소리」 「어둠」 등을 연이어 발표하며 문단의 주목을 받는다. 대학원 진학을 위해 서울로 거처를 옮긴 임철우는 「동행」 「직선과 독가스」 「불임기」 「사산하는 여름」 등을 발표한다. 1980년대 초반기의 한국 사회는 5월 광주는 물론 사회 비판이 절대적으로 인정되지 않는 표현 불허의 통제 사회였으나 임철우는 알레고리를 통해서나마 5월 광주를 증언하는 노력을 보인다. 등단 이래 단편을 꾸준히 발표한 임철우는 1984년에 창작집 『아버지의 땅』을 세상에 내놓게 되며 이 작품집으로 임철우는 제17회 한국일보창작문학상을 받는다.

임철우는 『아버지의 땅』에 뒤이어 『그리운 남쪽』을 1985년에 『달빛 밟기』를 1987년에 출간한다. 이처럼 꾸준하게 지속된 임철우의 단편 작업은 다시금 문단의 주목을 받게 되니, 1988년 임철우는 「붉은 방」으로 이상문학상을 받는다. 세상 도처에 무수히 깔린 가증스런 폭력과 거짓과 음모의 덫을 외면하지 않겠다는 임철우의 각별한 문학적 인식이 「붉은 방」이라는 탁월한 역작을 낳았고, 이 역작으로 임철우는 이상문학상 수상이라는 영예를 안게 된다.

1992년 잠시나마 제주도로 거처를 옮겨 『등대 아래서

soon May 1980 in Gwangju. Through his personal experience of the massacre in Gwangju, Lim Chul-woo would feel an infinite despair, as well as realize an endless love and faith, in humanity. Lim Chul-woo's literary works start from this love and faith.

In 1981, Lim Chul-woo debuted as a professional writer with "The Dog Thief" through the annual literary contest held by the *Seoul Shinmun*. From the year of his debut, Lim Chul-woo received the attention of the literary world by publishing "Their Dawn," "The Sound of the Wind in the Backyard," and "Darkness" in rapid succession. After moving to Seoul for graduate school, Lim Chul-woo published "Traveling Together," "Straight Lines and Poison Gas," "Period of Infertility," and "The Summer of Stillbirth." Although the Korean society of the early 1980s was a regulated one where social criticism, not to mention that of Gwangju of May, was absolutely forbidden to be expressed, Lim Chul-woo kept making attempts to testify about the Gwangju of May, albeit through allegory. After persistently putting out short stories since his literary debut, Lim Chul-woo published his first collection, *Father's Land*, in 1984, for which he received the 17th

휘파람』을 출간한 임철우는 1995년 한신대학교 문예창작학과 교수로 부임한다. 그런데 그는 제주도에서 『등대 아래서 휘파람』만을 쓰며 시간을 보낸 게 아니었다. 그는 그 섬에서 5월 광주의 절망과 희망, 상처와 화해의 대서사시라 할 『봄날』을 전력을 다해 집필했고 이 집필은 한신대학교 교수로 부임한 이후에도 지속된다. 『봄날』이 최종적으로 세상에 나온 건 1998년이다. 이로써 한국문학은 5월 광주에 대한 문학적 증언의 대미를 장식한다.

Annual *Hankook Ilbo* Creative Writing Award.

Following *Father's Land*, Lim Chul-woo published two more collections of short stories: *Longing for the South* in 1985, and *Stepping on the Moonlight* in 1987. With his continued work of short fictions, he garnered the attention of the literary world again, culminating with his winning the prestigious Yi Sang Literary Award in 1988 for "The Red Room." Lim Chul-woo's distinct literary awareness that would not ignore the reprehensible violence, falsity, and the trap of conspiracy spread abundantly all over the world gave birth to the masterpiece called "The Red Room," which brought him the honor of receiving the Yi Sang Literary Award.

After moving briefly to Jeju Island in 1992 and publishing *Whistling under the Lighthouse*, Lim Chul-woo became a professor in the Department of Creative Writing at Hanshin University in 1995. But *Whistling under the Lighthouse* was not the only work he wrote while in Jeju Island. On that island, he gave his full attention to *Spring Days*, which could be called a great epic of despair and hope, wound and reconciliation, regarding the Gwangju of May. Writing this work would continue after he started teaching at Hanshin University. It was in

1998 that *Spring Days* was finally published. With this work, Korean literature would mark a grand finale to literary testimony on the Gwangju of May 1980.

번역 크리스 최 Translated by Chris Choi

인문학자, 문화언어 컨설턴트. 매사추세츠 공대와 하버드에서 비교문학 박사 포함 총 네 개의 학위를 받았으며, 현재 뉴욕에 있는 컨설팅 펌 Educhora와 비영리단체인 Educhora Institute의 디렉터이다.

Chris Choi is apparently into balance. Bicultural and bilingual, she earned two degrees from M.I.T., then two more at Harvard, her final one a doctorate in Comparative Literature. As Director of Educhora, she researches, consults and facilitates learning on linguistic and cultural interaction, transition, fluency and impact. In addition to also directing the non-profit Educhora Institute, she spends time enjoying sports and fashion.

감수 전승희, 데이비드 윌리엄 홍
Edited by Jeon Seung-hee and David William Hong

전승희는 서울대학교와 하버드대학교에서 영문학과 비교문학으로 박사 학위를 받았으며, 현재 하버드대학교 한국학 연구소의 연구원으로 재직하며 아시아 문예 계간지 《ASIA》 편집위원으로 활동 중이다. 현대 한국문학 및 세계문학을 다룬 논문을 다수 발표했으며, 바흐친의 『장편소설과 민중언어』, 제인 오스틴의 『오만과 편견』 등을 공역했다. 1988년 한국여성연구소의 창립과 《여성과 사회》의 창간에 참여했고, 2002년부터 보스턴 지역 피학대 여성을 위한 단체인 '트랜지션하우스' 운영에 참여해 왔다. 2006년 하버드대학교 한국학 연구소에서 '한국 현대사와 기억'을 주제로 한 워크숍을 주관했다.

Jeon Seung-hee is a member of the Editorial Board of ASIA, is a Fellow at the Korea Institute, Harvard University. She received a Ph.D. in English Literature from Seoul National University and a Ph.D. in Comparative Literature from Harvard University. She has presented and published numerous papers on modern Korean and world literature. She is also a co-translator of Mikhail Bakhtin's *Novel and the People's Culture* and Jane Austen's *Pride and Prejudice*. She is a founding member of the Korean Women's Studies Institute and of the biannual Women's Studies' journal *Women and Society* (1988), and she has been working at 'Transition House', the first and oldest shelter for battered women in New England. She organized a workshop entitled "The Politics of Memory in Modern Korea" at the Korea Institute, Harvard University, in 2006. She also served as an advising committee member for the Asia-Africa Literature Festival in 2007 and for the POSCO Asian Literature Forum in 2008.

데이비드 윌리엄 홍은 미국 일리노이주 시카고에서 태어났다. 일리노이대학교에서 영문학을, 뉴욕대학교에서 영어교육을 공부했다. 지난 2년간 서울에서 거주하면서 처음으로 한국인과 아시아계 미국인 문학에 깊이 몰두할 기회를 가졌다. 현재 뉴욕에서 거주하며 강의와 저술 활동을 한다.

David William Hong was born in 1986 in Chicago, Illinois. He studied English Literature at the University of Illinois and English Education at New York University. For the past two years, he lived in Seoul, South Korea, where he was able to immerse himself in Korean and Asian-American literature for the first time. Currently, he lives in New York City, teaching and writing.

바이링궐 에디션 한국 현대 소설 018

직선과 독가스

2013년 6월 10일 초판 1쇄 인쇄 | 2013년 6월 15일 초판 1쇄 발행

지은이 임철우 | **옮긴이** 크리스 최 | **펴낸이** 방재석
감수 전승희, 데이비드 윌리엄 홍 | **기획** 정은경, 전성태, 이경재
편집 정수인, 이은혜, 이윤정 | **관리** 박신영 | **디자인** 이춘희

펴낸곳 아시아 | **출판등록** 2006년 1월 31일 제319-2006-4호
주소 서울특별시 동작구 흑석동 100-16
전화 02.821.5055 | **팩스** 02.821.5057 | **홈페이지** www.bookasia.org
ISBN 978-89-94006-73-4 (set) | 978-89-94006-76-5 (04810)
값은 뒤표지에 있습니다.

Bi-lingual Edition Modern Korean Literature 018
Straight Lines and Poison Gas

Written by Lim Chul-woo | **Translated by** Chris Choi
Published by Asia Publishers | 100-16 Heukseok-dong, Dongjak-gu, Seoul, Korea
Homepage Address www.bookasia.org | **Tel**. (822).821.5055 | **Fax**. (822).821.5057
First published in Korea by Asia Publishers 2013
ISBN 978-89-94006-73-4 (set) | 978-89-94006-76-5 (04810)